# PRETTY LIVES UGLY TRUTHS

**(BOOK 1)**

A Novel By

K. Elle Collier

## Thank You For Your Purchase

Great reviews mean everything to a writer. If you enjoyed this eBook in any way, please take a moment and go to Amazon and let me, and other readers, know what you thought. Once again, thank you and enjoy!

## Also by K. Elle Collier

My Man's Best Friend (Book 1)

Kai's Aftermath (Book 2)

Alana Bites Back (Book 3)

From Concept To Kindle

A Step-by-Step to Writing, Publishing and Marketing your Novel on the Amazon Kindle

**For more tips and a bunch of great stuff visit:**

www.modernwritingworks.com

http://www.kellecollier.com/

**Follow me on Twitter @K_ElleCollier**

**Like Me On Facebook - Author K. Elle Collier**

**PRETTY LIVES UGLY TRUTHS**



**Kindle Edition**

# Acknowledgements

Wow, what a journey this has been and it doesn't seem to be ending any time soon. First and foremost I would like to thank God, without his guidance and blessing none of this would be possible. There are so many people to thank and if I happen to not mention your name, please, please do not be offended, just have pity on me and my memory capacity. As always, I have to thank my family, your love and support continues to keep me moving forward with my passion. My sister from another mother, Kimberly Williams, love you more than you know, thank you for your continued love and support. To my awesome and speedy test readers, Ife Thomas, Derrick Jones, Jen Van Epps, Joyce Kenner, Lauren Brewton, Daneen Collier, Keno Redd, thank you all for your constructive feedback, I so greatly appreciate it. My Editor, Hope K. Farmby, for your time, understanding, and intuition to improve the quality of my work, you helped me see things I would have never seen. My copy editors, Rick Johnson and Emily Metzloff, thank you for making my work seamless and error free. Tiffany Tillman, Jonathan Reid and Jamila Daniel, my LA partners in crime, I love you guys. To my amazing fans, thank you for your continued support and positive feedback, you have made this journey so very enjoyable and I am forever grateful to you. As I love to say, keep reading and I promise to keep writing. Lastly, I cannot forget my ray of light that keeps me going every single day, that keeps me humble and grateful in every way, my beautiful and vivacious daughter Klarke, what would I do without you and how you have inspired me to be better than I could ever imagine. This is my fourth novel and second series that I have had the immense honor of sharing with you. My goal is to continue to keep bringing you the page-turners you love and enjoy reading as I cannot seem to stop writing them. :)

Thank you!
Until next time... Keep reading and I promise to keep writing ;)

~K. Elle

"*Writing is a dance with words, you start off slow and build to a beautiful rhythmic flow*" ~K. Elle

# Contents

***"Mistakes are always forgivable, if one has the courage to admit them"***

# Prologue

**November 18, 1993**
**10:05am on a Saturday**
**Los Angeles, CA**

"I never understood why the world loved my father so damn much."

Malcolm Monroe stood just inches from Langston Monroe's casket and stared down at his father's lifeless body. His pumpernickel skin and salt and pepper hair, a testament to the man's age and the life he lived.

At 16 years old, Malcolm knew a thing or two about death. He knew once you died, your soul went to heaven and your body went into the earth. He knew that everyone met their maker and judged you would be. Most of all, he knew on this day, the day of his father's funeral, he was glad his father was finally dead.

A gloomy LA morning coupled with a cold November day was the perfect backdrop for a funeral. A procession of black town cars and one hearse slowly traveled down Barham Blvd before turning onto Forest Lawn Drive. The dark clouds parted as a brief downfall of rain let everyone know the storm wasn't through soaking the slick streets below.

The rain pellets drummed like chubby fists on the hoods of the long line of black town cars accented with silver trim.

Malcolm and his two siblings rode in silence, vulnerable to the movement from the motion of the car and the road beneath them. Lance, 14, brave but still clearly intimidated by the crowds, and Lacey, 12, innocent enough to most of the world, detached to the events surrounding her.

A faint smile drifted across Malcolm's face as he glanced up at his mother sitting in the front seat. Eleanor Monroe sat tall and regal, her head high but her spirits low. She turned toward her eldest son, and their eyes connected, receiving his faint smile, until turning back around, wiping a tear away.

Malcolm's smile faded as he turned to vacuously stare out the window at the multitude of people that lined the soaked streets to pay their respects. They were cloaked in colorful parkas, rain coats and more. Many also held umbrellas to shield themselves from the wet rain.

They came from miles and stood for hours to say their last goodbyes to a legend gone too soon. Sad eyes, eager eyes, all of whom were there to desperately try and catch a glimpse of what remained of the man they still mourned for and cried for. They huddled together in groups, still unable to grasp that Langston Wade Monroe was gone.

Langston Wade Monroe wasn't just a legendary singer/songwriter, he was the man everyone listened to growing up. A man who came from nothing and rose to become one of the greatest musicians of all time. The man who influenced countless other groups that came after him.

The man who revolutionized the music industry with his unique flare and style. He was adored and praised all over the world. He was an icon, a husband and a brother. He was a father to his family, but an adversary to himself.

And now... he was dead.

Malcolm closed his eyes and replayed that crazed day and unforgettable moment of the very instant he learned his father was gone. He recalled the feeling of how he knew that everything would change and how he and his family would never be the same. He replayed the reporter's voice in his head, how it was strong, informative, baffled and sad. It was a voice that Malcolm would never forget… a feeling he would always remember.

*"Today, November 10th, the world is in shock as we are now hearing the news of the death of legendary singer-songwriter and musician Langston Monroe. It was confirmed minutes ago that Monroe was found dead in his Bel Air home, with an apparent gunshot wound to the head.*

*Langston Monroe was an American musician who helped shape the sound of Uptown Records in the 1970's with a string of hits including, "The Way You Make Me Feel," "Be Safe and Sound" and "Beneath the Beautiful." Shock and devastation are the words that are running through the music world on this day, (pause) shock and devastation… to the music world and millions of fans around the world, Langston Monroe will be missed… a legend…"*

The reporter's words faded as Malcolm was brought back to his present. The town car slowly turned the corner leading to *Forest Lawn Cemetery* and carefully drove through the double steel green gates. The grounds were massive, acres of freshly cut green grass with small headstones marking each spot of a life gone. The procession of cars behind them lined the road like carefully placed dominos. Each car filled with family, friends, and music industry colleagues.

The rain continued to fall, harder than before, as if the devil himself was trying to make a statement. Malcolm looked over at his siblings, their eyes connecting and going their separate ways, each of them lost in their own personal thoughts and individual reflections.

The procession of cars finally arrived at the burial site. The car doors opened and everyone quickly took shelter under the black blanket of umbrellas.

The Monroe family stood surrounding the copper and gold casket that laid before them. The rain washed over the casket leaving a glistening reflection as the pellets slid off one by one. There, they said their last farewells to a father who'd been the focal point of their lives, a musician who walked to the beat of his own drum, a man that no one ever understood, but worked to love him anyway.

As Langton's body slowly made its last decent into the dark and saturated ground, Malcolm closed his eyes and prayed to the God above. Malcolm squeezed his eyes so tight that he saw a multitude of lights before him. It was within those lights that he proclaimed within himself - *Please God, please make my father pay for everything that he's done.*

# ONE

**November 17, 2013**
**Friday, 8:05am**

***Twenty Years Later...***

Alex Monroe woke to a sensual touch that was sending shivers through her naked body. She opened her eyes to see her husband of seven years, Malcolm Monroe, looking down at her.

He smiled, seeing her finally wake.

"Good morning, birthday girl."

"Good morning to *you*," Alex breathed out as she turned onto her back to face him as Malcolm's six foot one frame hovered over hers. Alex reached up as she slinked her hand down his dark, hair-covered chest, going from right to left, taking it all in as she felt his erect nipples rise beneath her touch.

"It's about to get even better," Malcolm said as he continued on his morning mission. He leaned down over her, and slowly and methodically rained kisses down her neck, chest and stomach. Alex let out a soft moan as a smile danced across her face.

"What are you doing to me?" Alex whispered, feeling her wetness waking up and taking over.

Malcolm licked his full lips and smiled once again, this one a devious one. "Look at it as an early birthday surprise. You do like surprises don't you?" Malcolm asked. Without waiting for an answer, he slid his left hand under her bare brown ass and slowly parted her legs with his.

Alex felt his hardness against her thigh as she closed her eyes and bit her bottom lip. She felt his other hand slide down her stomach making soft circles around her naval before heading down to her love box, separating her soft lips with his thumb, spreading her juices that were overflowing all around her throbbing labia.

Alex whined as her body began to move in a slow rhythmic synch lead by his fingers. She braced herself for what she knew would come as she reached out taking ahold of their cream colored satin sheets, a fist full in each hand as she took a deep breath, trying to relax, not wanting to come just yet. But it was hard..., so very hard.

Malcolm slid his body down, dropped his head between her legs as he found the most sensitive spot on her clit, then proceeded to feather lick it, tease it and suck it like a ripe peach on a hot summer's day before sliding his fingers in her, slowly searching for *that* spot.

Alex's body continued to respond with every move Malcolm made, moving with every twist of his hand until he found it, her G-spot. Alex's body did one quick jolt and felt like she hit the ceiling as Malcolm proceeded to devour her like a tiger with his prey.

"Yes, baby, mmmm..." Alex moaned out.

She felt her climax racing to the finish line as if it were running a 40-meter dash in under five seconds flat. Her breath erratic and shallow, she knew it was only a matter of time before it was over. One last shutter of sensation before an abundance of colors flashed before her eyes.

Alex squeezed her eyes shut as she enjoyed the array of sensation accompanied by a self-made kaleidoscope that danced before her vision as her body made one last involuntary convulsion before she floated back down to the other side. Alex held still, very still, enjoying her fall into that place of refuge, that place of peace, that place of pure bliss. She smiled.

Alex continued to lay still, soaking in the moment but wanting more, wanting to feel Malcolm inside of her, wanting to take a part of him with her. Not wanting to let him go, not just yet.

Alex took a deep breath and made it her mission to stay in the moment, waiting for more... of him. She waited, eyes closed, anticipation high, until an unfamiliar sound, a crackling paper sound, prompted her eyes open to witness something she could not believe. Malcolm was sliding on a condom. Alex sat up a little taller, tilted her head to the side, her eyebrow arching up on cue, as she thought to herself, *Am I seeing what I think I am seeing?*

Alex held her composure, not trying to jump to any conclusions. “Malcolm, honey, what are you doing?” Alex asked, her tone calm, her thoughts on the tip of brewing out of control.

Malcolm stopped, mid-roll, and looked up at his wife. “I’m putting on a condom.”

"Yes, I can see that," Alex said as she quickly sat all the way up on her butt, taking a deep breath, "But…why?"

Malcolm let out a small chuckle, "Baby, it's not like that."

Malcolm continued to roll the condom the rest of the way down his erect shaft.

Alex forced out a smile, a defense mechanism that *normally* used to keep her calm. "Like what?" She questioned, trying not to let her thoughts overtake her composure.

"Like what you're thinking," Malcolm threw back.

"Well… what I'm thinking is that you're a married man and you're buying condoms?"

"I didn't *buy* them, I got 'em from Lance... my brother."

Alex's forced smile became even broader. "Yeah, I know who your brother is Malcolm. Okay, let me rephrase it, why do *YOU* have them?"

Malcolm stopped what he was doing and looked up at Alex. "I'm just trying to be safe."

"Safe?"

"Yeah safe, you stopped taking the pill because of your blood pressure medication, so… you know… I don't want to have any…accidents."

Alex raised *both* eyebrows this time. *Am I hearing all this correctly?* Alex cleared her throat, took a deep breath, trying to calm herself, "Accidents… as in an accidental pregnancy?"

"Well…" Malcolm rubbed the back of his neck, "yeah."

"Really?" Alex looked away and shook her head. *This is not happening, not this morning, not the morning of my 40th birthday.* Alex took another slow, deep breath, then a second one since the first one hadn't accomplished anything.

"Malcolm, I'm forty years old *today* and I think it's time, no correction, past time to start thinking about having a child."

Malcolm rubbed the back of his neck again as he looked down at the bed he sat on, then back up. Alex knew as far as Malcolm was concerned, his career as a filmmaker came first, and having a family second. He wanted everything to be perfect before he even thought about starting a family; Alex, on the other hand, had a different plan. She wanted a family and after waiting seven years she was determined to get it by any means necessary. She was tired of waiting for that perfect time to have a child, as Malcolm diplomatically put it. In life there was no perfect time and accidents do happen. The time was now.

Malcolm sat back on his heels, running his fingers through his loosely twisted locks, "Are we having this conversation now?"

Alex grabbed the sheets bunched under them, pulling them over her bare legs, "I think we should have this conversation at some point."

Malcolm breathed out his building frustrations, "I just don't think having a child right now is… the *best* thing."

"Why not?" Alex said, feeling a sense of deja vu all over again.

"Well for starters, I just dumped the majority of my money into shooting my last film which means we can't afford a child right now."

Alex took a deep breath, "I don't know why you worry so much about money."

"I worry because nothing in this business is guaranteed. If I don't get distribution for this film, I'm fucked. And not in a good way."

"I make enough to float us for a while until you..."

"See there you go again, I don't need my wife supporting us."

"Then maybe it's time to start thinking about switching gears."

Malcolm ran his hand down the side of his cheek, scratching his five o'clock shadow. Annoyance spread over his face quicker than a deliberately set brush fire on a hot California day.

"Are you really saying this to me right now, after all I have been through to get my film to this point?"

"Baby, I'm just being realistic, one of us has to be." Alex couldn't stop the words from tumbling out of her mouth. She knew what she said would sting, sting hard and instantly regretted every syllable associated with it.

"Wow." Malcolm gave Alex a wrathful glare. They stared at each other, each furious in their own way. Alex watched her husband start a slow burn.

"Malcolm I…"

"No. How dare you say that shit to me?" Malcolm swung his legs off the bed, sitting on the edge, then looking back at Alex. "I am a filmmaker period and I'm sorry if you can't accept that…"

Malcolm stood, pulling on his shorts and didn't finish his statement. He didn't need to. Alex was smart enough to fill in the blanks.

Alex quickly retreated, "Malcolm, baby, that's not what I'm saying… it just seems like you have been banging your head up against a wall without any results for a long time and…I was just thinking..."

Alex paused, struck by what she thought might be the spark of a good idea. Maybe even something that could lessen the blow she just hurled at him. "I could call my father. He'd love to have you come help run his construction company."

Malcolm shot Alex a sidelong glance that said more than just *get the fuck outta here.*

"Really Alex? That would be just fantastic. The thought of working for your dad really makes my dick hard."

Alex bit down on her lip, feeling as if she was sinking… fast. She reached for one last branch that might stop her descent, "It doesn't have to be permanent, just something to bring in some extra income until something happens for you… for us." Alex said, quickly correcting herself.

Malcolm laughed to himself, shaking his head. "Why don't you just say it Alex? You don't believe I can do this."

Alex knew his words were coming from a place of disappointment, discouragement and his defeated ego. She knew his journey as a filmmaker had been paralyzing and intimidating. It was a roller-coaster heading down a steep hill from which he was unable to stop or jump off.

"That's not true. I've always supported you, always," Alex pleaded. She felt herself becoming emotional as her desperate attempts to gain forgiveness were greeted with a coldness that could rival the arctic.

Malcolm shook his head, "Well if you did Alex, we wouldn't be having this conversation now, now would we?"

They stared at each other again, this time, the moments growing more uncomfortable the longer they didn't speak. It was one that filled with issues from the past that always seemed to creep into the present. Alex was quiet, and unable to speak. She was unable to save everything that was lost in this moment.

"Exactly," Malcolm shot back.

Alex closed her eyes as the last three years of their marriage rushed to the forefront of her mind. She thought about how most of their disagreements started after Malcolm's first attempt to make a film had failed miserably. The knife had been twisted since it had been something that everyone expected to do well and put him on the map. Instead, its failure was his and had thrown his career way off course.

From that point, their life as a couple only got worse. The days became less blissful, emphasizing that familiar saying, "Marriage is hard work and anyone who thinks differently is single."

Alex was determined to make it work. She was in it for the long haul. Alex yearned to have a family, something she deeply desired that would make her life feel complete, something that Malcolm promised her when he took his vows in front of 200 of their closest friends and family, something Alex never had growing up.

"Baby, I am *sooo* sorry, I didn't mean to hurt you or disparage your career. I just want us to be happy."

Malcolm continued to look down towards the ground as if he were studying something, "Us or you?"

"Us... *us*," Alex emphasized.

Malcolm looked up briefly locking eyes with Alex then turning back away.

"I don't want to fight, I love you and I want to work through this, together, all of this," Alex said in a pleading tone.

"Alex you know how important my career is but somehow you always seem to slam it, in turn you are slamming me," he said, sounding miserable.

Alex hated when he said those words to her. She hated the thought that she didn't believe in him, because she did, she so did. That was why she loved him so much.

"Malcolm," she said looking up at him, "I do believe in you and your career."

"Then why do you say the things that you say?"

Alex stared deep into Malcolm's eyes, looking for a sliver of hope for forgiveness, "I guess that's just my way of helping."

"Well you have a shitty way of showing it." His eyes filled with anger once again as they narrowed, staring at her. "Thanks for ruining our morning. Happy *fucking* birthday..."

He turned and stormed off, heading for the bathroom.

"Malcolm wait, please."

Alex's last words were met with a slammed door and an empty feeling.

"Dammit." Alex laid back on her pillow, and felt her heart sink five inches into her chest. She knew Malcolm's outburst was filled with more than just his career not going well. She knew it also had to do with the upcoming anniversary of the death of his dad, Langston Monroe, twenty years ago, tomorrow. A legendary singer the world never wanted to forget. To Malcolm, Langston Monroe was a man he tried to never remember.

Alex hated when they fought. No, that wasn't right, she hated to fight period. She wrapped her arms around her legs, pulling them close to her chest, trying to think of what to say and what to do to make this moment better. She mentally scolded herself for even bringing up his stalled career today, but couldn't stop herself from having that selfish moment when she wanted it to be all about her. She had needs too after all.

Alex took a huge stress-filled sigh as she released her vocals throughout the empty bedroom, "damn, damn, damn it!"

She swung her legs off the bed, stood as she grabbed her robe and headed to the *closed* bathroom door.

Alex stopped, listened for a moment and gathered her thoughts. She needed a plan of action so she could figure out exactly the right thing to say. Where to start and where the conversation should end.

She gathered all her strength and raised her fist to knock, before quickly dropping it down to her side. She laid her forehead against the door, and rocked back and forth. This was harder than she imagined, but it had to be done, she reminded herself.

Alex slowly turned the doorknob, hearing it squeak as it opened to see Malcolm standing by the sink, setting up his utensils to shave. Alex took another deep breath and managed to unglue her feet from the doorway as she slowly walked over to where Malcolm was standing.

She stood inches behind him and saw his eyes in the mirrored reflection catch hers. She took that as encouragement and slid her arms through his, around his waist. She pressed her face against his bare back and felt his body go stiff to her touch. Alex didn't care if he wasn't forgiving her yet, she was standing her ground. She squeezed him a bit tighter, smelling his morning scent, loving the fact that her man always smelled so good.

They stood in silence as their bodies swayed a bit from their natural momentum. Alex breathed him in once again, this time gaining a bit of courage for what had to be done and what had to be said. On her exhale she lovingly proclaimed her apologies, "Baby, I'm sorry, I wasn't thinking, I know tomorrow is…"

Malcolm's body stayed stiff as he continued to look down, continued to organize his morning shaving utensils.

Alex looked up towards the mirror; she continued to stare at him until he looked back up, caught Malcolm's eyes, "…kind of an important day for you and your family."

Malcolm just looked away, back to what he was doing. "Alex, I really don't want to talk about it."

Alex dropped her eyes, pressing her face deeper into his back, into his soul. Her chin, nestled in his back, rose and fell with his inhale and exhale. She wasn't letting him go, not yet, not until she felt that *they* were okay.

"I think you should. It's the 20th anniversary."

Malcolm pulled away from Alex, turning around to face her, "Right, twenty years that my legendary father is dead, so what do you want me to do, Alex? Cry? Scream? Shout out in anger to the mountain tops above? What Alex, what do you want me to do?"

Alex stared deep into Malcolm's eyes but said nothing.

She swallowed hard, letting out a slow sigh.

Malcolm turned back to the sink, filling his hand with shaving cream, slathering it all over his right and left cheek. Normally, he was meticulous with his shaving, but today was different. She could see he was letting his emotions over his father's death get the best of him. Alex stayed quiet, very quiet. She knew Malcolm didn't like to talk about his dad. He never spoke about the time he spent with him, or talked about the fact that the man was a legend. Matter of fact, none of his children did. Not Malcolm, nor his brother Lance or sister Lacey. They were the type of family that swept despair under the beautiful rugs which were laid across their lives, pretending like their problems never existed or even ever mattered.

"I just thought... just thought if you talked about it, it might help you deal with some of the things that bothered you."

"Alex please stop treating me like I'm one of your goddamn patients."

"I'm just trying to help."

"If you want to help, just let me do me and I will let you do you." Malcolm picked up his razor and began to shave.

"Malcolm I-"

Malcolm raised his hand, stopping Alex from finishing what she wanted to say, what she needed to get out. "Seriously, it's cool, I gotta get ready for this meeting today."

Alex took a step back, feeling the frustration engulf her body. But, after seven years of marriage, she knew when to stop, when to step down, and when to take a time out.

"Right, the distribution meeting for your movie. I'll let you do… you."

Alex turned, about to head out the bathroom, but as a woman she had to try one last angle, one last way to penetrate her husband's wall of steel, still searching for a back door into his emotions, "Do you need any help with my birthday dinner tonight?"

"Nope. Got it all under control," Malcolm replied in a cold tone, continuing to stare at his reflection, carefully gliding the blade down his cheek with a steady hand.

"Okay," Alex looked down then back up, "great." She stared at her husband, hoping to get one last glance that might tell her that he was okay and more importantly, that they were okay. She waited, but there was nothing as he concentrated on shaving. Alex waited for a few more moments before finally turning and walking out the bathroom, a tear falling down her face.

# TWO

Sylvia Batista stirred from the sound of her cell phone ringing on the antique white night stand beside her. Half awake, she peeked out from under her white satin mask covering her eyes at the digital clock that read in big fat, red numbers. *4:45am? Really?? Who's calling this early?*

She sighed and emerged from underneath her two-toned feathered down duvet cocoon she liked to call her bed. One swift yank and her mask was around her neck as she sat up to lean against her ivory cushioned headboard.

While Sylvia understood the 24-hour a day nature of her business as a publicist, she didn't have to love it. She leaned over and swiped the lock screen on her white iPhone from the night stand and saw that it was her assistant calling. She groaned and hit accept.

"This better be good."

"Oh, you're gonna love this," her assistant Vanessa chimed back, mirroring Sylvia's obvious annoyance. At 4:45 in the morning, it was to be expected.

Sylvia lowered her tired eyes as she took a deep breath preparing herself for the worst. But 24-hour access was what you got when you hired the top publicist in Los Angeles. Sylvia's client list boasted a wide variety of top talent in everything from entertainment-like movies and television to sports.

Unfortunately, that meant a never-ending revolving series of crises and fires that her famous clients loved to start. That also meant she always needed to be ready at a moment's notice and never take a break.

It was a challenge to be sure, but that was what Sylvia lived for and made her tick. It was a job she was born to do and she knew she wanted to do ever since she could remember. She had realized at a young age that she had negotiation skills far above and beyond her young peers.

If she didn't get what she wanted when she was a child, Sylvia Batista didn't cry or throw a tantrum, she simply figured out how to get what she wanted and found a new strategy to go after it. When college presented itself, she decided that the law school route was the most practical use of her skills, and was eventually able to parlay that into the more glamorous and exciting field of public relations. It was a career she had been very successful at.

She wouldn't admit to how tough the job was, but she would brag about how there wasn't anyone else who could do it with the same precision and ease.

That's why they called her.

"Okay, let's hear it."

"Lance Monroe was arrested last night three miles from his home."

Sylvia opened her eyes as they rolled to the back of her head hanging on for dear life. "Of course he was."

Lance Monroe was the outspoken ex-pro athlete turned ESPN commentator and a royal pain in Sylvia's ass. Not only was he an ex-client, he was also her soon to be ex-husband.

It had been love at first sight. Sylvia knew from the beginning that saying "I do" to Lance would be the bane of her existence, and she had been right - for more than one reason.

He had said all the right things. Worked above and beyond what any normal man in his position would have to earn her heart, but at the end of the day, he did and she couldn't say no; she was in love, in love with her best friend. Unfortunately that wasn't enough to keep her around; Lance had his own agenda, one that Sylvia was not down for at all.

"So why are you calling me?"

"His lawyers left a message on our service a few hours ago. Apparently Lance requested you and only you."

Sylvia shook her head thinking how it had been much easier to get rid of Lance when they were still together. Way easier.

Sylvia and Lance's divorce was close to being finalized as soon as Lance signed the papers and Sylvia couldn't have been happier. Unfortunately, it seemed every time she looked up, Lance was right there pulling her back in, not to mention prolonging the situation.

Sylvia knew she needed to put a stop to this and needed to find a way to get Lance out of her life for good. She just needed to find the strength to do it.

"While I'm flattered as well as incredibly annoyed, please call his lawyers back and let them know that I will pass."

"Pass?"

"Yes, pass."

"But he's your husband."

An annoyed smile skipped across Sylvia's face, "He is, but soon he will be my EX. Let's not lose perspective here."

"Right… well do you at least want to know what happened?"

"If I cared?"

"You don't care?" Vanessa said with a hint of sympathy mixed in.

Sylva slowly shook her head as she felt a mounting nausea building in her stomach. She swallowed…hard, hoping whatever was trying to come up stayed down.

"Fine, I'll humor you," Sylvia said.

"Driving under the influence."

Sylvia laughed out loud as she raked her fingers through her dark black hair with perfectly (and costly) appointed highlights, twirling the ends with her index finger.

"Ya know, you would *think* if you made way over a million dollars a year to sit on your ass and talk trash you could spend a couple thousand on a driver when you want to go out and party."

"Yeah, that's way too easy. But, there's more."

Sylvia stopped laughing as she heard the serious tone in her assistant's voice.

"What else?"

"Kidnapping."

"Kidnapping?"

"Apparently the woman he was with is claiming that Lance forced her into his car unwillingly."

Sylvia dropped her hand down to her lap, "Wow."

"We both know that he is going to need someone to spin the hell out of this if he wants to save his career as a commentator."

"Something he should have thought about before this all went down," Sylvia breathed out fatigue and frustration. It was way too early for this.

"So what now?"

"He's been in jail since 2am. They won't start accepting bail until 7am," Vanessa continued.

"Yeah, that's unfortunate, but it's what you get when you take a hostage."

Vanessa chuckled at Sylvia's familiar sarcasm.

Sylvia glanced back at her clock, "I hope he brought a good book to read."

"Should I call his lawyers and tell them you will take the case?"

Sylvia paused for a moment, wincing slightly from the nausea and weighed the benefits of representing him and what she might gain to spin this catastrophe into his favor. The answer hit her like bullet train. Absolutely nothing.

"No."

"No?"

"No. He's gonna have to pull himself out of this one his own self."

Sylvia hit end on her phone before Vanessa had a chance to convince her otherwise. She shook her head and stared around her monotone colored bedroom. She loved her room, loved the colors, and especially loved the feel. Lance had hated the colors in their home. He always joked telling her that her Spanish culture was not revealed in her decorating style.

*Screw him, I like my style. It's simple, sleek, and elegant* - at least that's what she told herself. She took a deep breath, and thought once again about how much she despised Lance and how he would never let her live this down. She also thought about how out of character this was for him. There had to be more to this story, much more.

Sylvia placed her phone back down onto her night stand and slid back down under the covers. Then something hit her like a bullet out of an AK-47. She sat up, grabbing her phone and hit her calendar icon to check the date: November 9.

Her mind quickly populated the memories making sense of the situation at hand. She sighed loudly cursing to herself, "Never fails. Every year… every freakin' year."

Sylvia knew how much Lance loved and admired his father. But she also knew just how much pain the man had caused him.

Sylvia shook her head, trying to shake that tiny voice of morality. She tried to shoo it away where she wouldn't care about his problems.

She hated feeling like this. That "I-know-I-should-help-him-but-he-makes-me-so-damn-mad feeling."

She turned, trying to ignore that voice inside her and pulled her satin pillow over her head, burying her face deep into the pillow, hoping it might muffle the voices coming from inside.

Nope, Nada. Nothing.

She hated the pull Lance had over her, even now after their short lived marriage. She hated that she still loved him even after all that he did to her, just hated it.

She threw the pillow to the side, sat back up in her bed, rested her head again on her cushioned ivory headboard. Her mind drifted back to the day Lance walked into her office and straight into her life…

*Sylvia was having her usual hectic day. E-mails after e-mail, not to mention the demanding clients with plenty of phone calls to return. She remembered looking up from the chaos in front of her to see Lance Monroe standing there as if he just stepped out of a GQ magazine photo shoot. The first thing that skipped across her mind was pictures did not do him justice. He was wearing a tan suit, pink tie and crisp white shirt from what she recalled.*

*He was tall, very tall, six-five easy with a nicely chiseled body that Michelangelo could have easily sculpted. He had been referred to her agency by a client who had told her that he was an athlete that needed a boost in his career, needed some heat around him, a fresh start. Those were all the words that excited Sylvia and made her tick.*

*Lance took three steps her way as he flashed that infectious smile – something she used to love, but now hated with a passion. It's amazing how the things that once attracted you to a person ended up being the most annoying things in the end.*

*"You must be Sylvia Batista, I have heard nothing but rave reviews about your work," Lance said, flashing his million-dollar smile, and with as much as he was making, was a legitimate estimate of its worth.*

*Sylvia studied Lance's face just as diligently as she had studied his portfolio, his hazel eyes and soft brown skin blended together like a well-made cappuccino.*

*Lance started his career in football a star running back from UCLA and had gone as a first round draft pick to the Chicago Bears before being traded to the San Francisco 49'ers. It was there that he distinguished himself by racking up a career high of rushing yards as well as a laundry list of legal accusations that ranged from drunk driving to public disturbances.*

*Lance had issues, issues from his past that impeded and disrupted his future as a star football player. Sylvia had been hired to fix the damage he had already caused, but unfortunately, she had no idea the extent of the internal damage that had already been done.*

*Sylvia still remembered that day as if it were yesterday, and despite that being ten years ago, it seemed that Lance still had not learned his lesson.*

Sylvia was yanked from her flashback with another wave of nausea that landed her on her feet moving quickly to the bathroom. Sylvia dropped to her knees and watched as everything she ate last night was no longer a part of her.

She sat back on the heels, holding the rim of the toilet as she reached out for a tissue to wipe her mouth. She definitely needed to lay back down if she expected to halfway function today. She glanced at the clock that sat over her double glass mirrors and saw it was now 5:15. She had a good hour before she needed to head down to the courthouse to make it by 7am.

Sylvia rose and took a few steps over to the sink grabbing the mouthwash. She twisted off the cap and took a long swig. She placed the bottle down and looked at the reflection staring back at her.

Sylvia Batista knew leaving Lance had been the right thing to do. She just hadn't expected to find out that she was seven weeks pregnant the day she filed the divorce papers.

# THREE

"Is that what you are wearing to your meeting?" Randolph Sanders watched as his fiancée, Lacey Monroe got dressed for the day.

Lacey glanced down at what she was wearing: a fitted pencil line skirt that stopped mid-thigh accompanied with a pristine white, low-cut button-up Donna Karen blouse with matching three-inch heels. *Seemed perfectly fine to me*, she thought.

Lacey turned to face Randolph and stared at his caramel colored face with light freckles admiring his handsome face. She tilted her head, giving him the sweetest smile she could muster.

"I think it's fine. Besides, it's what my fans like, so I have to portray that at all times," Lacey said, as she swung back around, glancing in the mirror one final time, now admiring how *she* looked.

Randolph shifted his five foot ten inch frame from side to side, and ran his hand down his cobalt blue tie with yellow diamonds, before tucking it into the pants pocket of his dark tan suit.

"Well your fans have to understand that you are about to become the First Lady of Woodland Hills Baptist Church. First Ladies don't dress like that."

Lacey stared at her *newly* engaged fiancée and smiled. She wondered why she tolerated him and his conservative ways and realized it was because he worshiped the ground she walked on. That had been enough for her to say "Yes."

At age 32, Lacey knew it was time to settle down and maybe even start a family, and who would be better than to do that with than the good Pastor Randolph Sanders of Woodland Hills Baptist Church.

Randolph wasn't just any pastor, he was a very well-known one. In fact, he led one of the largest Baptist churches in Woodland Hills, CA boasting a congregation of over 2000 members each of whom idolized each and every word that came from his mouth. He was a leader and a good man. A man of non-judgment who always acknowledged that no one was perfect. Lacey loved his leadership qualities and of course his good looks didn't hurt, but mostly, she loved what he represented for her - stability.

Every woman wanted stability in her life, at least the smart ones did, as Lacey always said. Lacey reminded herself of the stability Randolph gave her. Stability was something that she had lost very young in life, and she'd have given anything to have it again.

Lacey and Randolph were as opposite as they could get. She was an R&B singer with a larger than life diva personality that grew out of the shadow of her legendary father, Langston Monroe. While Randolph on the other hand was Georgian born and raised in the church. As far as Lacey was concerned, he was gonna save her, he just didn't know it yet.

Lacey turned and walked three steps towards her fiancée. "Please don't tell me you are going to be one of those controlling husbands. I can't deal with that, not at all, so let me know now please, so I can run for the hills," Lacey said with a half-serious smile.

"Baby you know I'm not that way, but there's an image you have to uphold."

"And how do you expect me to do that when my image as an R&B singer is sultry sexy, not casual conservative? I have to compete with Beyoncé."

Randolph laughed and pulled Lacey closer to him and gave her a quick peck on the lips, "Beyoncé has nothing on you."

"Oh yeah… well tell that to her millions of fans."

"I'm sure we can find a happy medium. What do you think?"

Lacey let a meaningful smile play across her face and figured she may as well tell him what he wanted to hear instead of how she really felt. She was learning the art of quiet compromise, a trait, she had picked up at 32, and usually was something needed in a relationship.

"That could be arranged," Lacey shot back primly.

Randolph smiled broadly and gave Lacey another kiss on the lips. He had been asking Lacey to marry him for two months and she had finally said yes after only six months of dating.

He didn't need six months to know that Lacey was the woman who should be his wife. He knew that the moment he first laid eyes on her at the Essence festival in New Orleans.

He had been there with his church celebrating their 5-year anniversary and Lacey had come down to perform backup vocals as a favor for her longtime friend Jill Scott. Lacey had a small but loyal following of her own in the music industry, a following that began to build once people found out who her late father was.

Lacey had every intention to make it without the help of her father's name, but she still had a ways to go before she could sell out a huge arena. Her voice and talent was still a bit underdeveloped, something she would change once her next album dropped. She'd finally connected with a top producer who had figured out her style and vocal range. After writing three hits for her, it was time for Lacey Monroe to shine.

"So I have an idea," Lacey leaned in and planted a soft kiss on her fiancée's mouth. She nibbled on his bottom lip before making her way to the top.

"Okay, I'm listening," Randolph breathed out between tiny kisses.

"Well, I have some time before my meeting with my producers and I just thought…" Lacey took a deep breath as she slid her tongue inside his mouth as she pressed her body against his. Lacey let out a low moan as their tongues became lost and tangled in each other.

Lacey pulled back, licked her moist lips, "I just thought that maybe we could forget about that silly promise of…."

"No," Randolph said in a firm tone as he pulled away even further.

"Honey, I need it, I need you," Lacey continued as she placed her lips against his, as she ran her fingers over his nipple, feeling it rise through his shirt.

Randolph pulled back, "Okay, that's enough."

Lacey let out a soft whine as she slid her hand down his chest and around his waist, "Baby?"

Randolph sighed as he placed his hands over hers, removing them from his waist and taking a big step back, "We promised to take a vow of celibacy until we got married."

"You're the one who promised. I just nodded my head."

"Which in turn is your promise."

A frustrated Lacey sighed loudly, "I don't understand why we have to wait."

"Should I remind you that in Thessalonians 4:3-5: *It is God's will that we should be sanctified; that we should avoid sexual immorality; that each of us should learn to control our own bodies in a way that is holy and honorable, not in passion just like the pagans, who do not know God.*"

Lacey dropped her head. She knew that marrying a pastor might come with some… well, adjustments to her lifestyle. They were adjustments she was having a hard time… well, adjusting too.

"Why can't you just look at it as a… test drive… before you sign on the dotted line?" Lacey asked as she took a few steps closer to Randolph wrapping her arms around him once again. Once again he removed her hands.

"It is tempting yes, but I know God would not bring me a wife who could not satisfy me in bed."

Lacey was relentless and usually not one for taking "no" for an answer. Even as a child that had been her downfall. If she wanted something, she went after it with everything she had and everything she could muster up. She wasn't used to being restricted or rejected.

Lacey's lips found Randolph's once again as her body moved in for one last try, her mouth connected with his as her tongue pushed deep inside, tasting every part of his mouth, his softness, his warmth.

"Lacey, we have to stop."

"We are only kissing."

"Well kissing can lead to other things..."

"Did I tell you how much I liked other things?" Lacey went back in and her lips began their decent, starting with Randolph's neck, then chest. She smiled as she felt his manhood growing and expanding by the second.

"I missed you baby, and I know you missed me," Lacey said as she rubbed her hand down his stomach over his belt and around his rising manhood before turning her body and pressing her round ass hard against him, swaying from left to right and back again.

A low satisfying groan came from deep down inside her man's core. Lacey knew Randolph was a man of God, but he was a *man* first.

Lacey smiled as Randolph succumbed to her sexual advances by ravenously grabbing her hips and rocking them back and forth. He picked up speed and rhythm with each sway.

She felt success building on her side as she smiled then grabbed his right hand and slid it under her panty-less skirt and between her thighs. Randolph moaned and Lacey shuttered as his fingers came alive. He glided up her vagina separating her wet throbbing lips as he circled her growing clit, spreading her juices from north to south, east then west.

"Yes, baby, that's how I like it, I want you so badly..." she turned quickly, covering his mouth with hers, their kiss was deep with passion... overflowing even. They definitely had undeniable chemistry and no bible verse would stop them now.

Lacey felt his manhood getting harder and bigger as she reached down to unbuckle his pants. Her hands shook with anticipation of what she had been wanting and yearning, to get for months and now, she was about to get what she desperately needed.

Lacey felt Randolph's hand push hers with hardened force, "**NO**!" Randolph shouted as the force propelled her back from him, hard, too hard.

She fell back, hitting the dresser drawers, knocking everything on it, off of it, before tumbling down to the floor. She shook her head, glanced up at him and thought to herself, he had clearly lost his ever loving mind.

"What the hell is wrong with you?" Lacey said as she gathered herself, trying to get up, but quickly losing her balance, still winded from the fall.

Randolph raced over to help her up, "I'm so sorry, are you hurt?" Randolph grabbed Lacey's hand before she yanked it away.

"I'm fine." Lacey slowly stood, regained her composure but her anger was brewing like a black kettle on a wood fire stove.

"We should pray," Randolph said to her in an apologetic voice.

Lacey took a deep breath, turned, opened the top dresser drawer, and pulled out a pair of purple panties before turning back towards her fiancé and giving him a less than loving look, "You pray, I have a get to my meeting."

Lacey gave Randolph one last withering look before grabbing her purse and heading out the door, panties in hand.

Lacey walked down the stairs, as she heard her name being called. She continued to walk, ignoring her future husband's pleas for forgiveness. She headed out the glass stained double doors of their home and walked over to her white two-door Lexus, equipped with a sun roof and butter colored seats sitting in their spiral driveway.

Lacey clenched her teeth before taking a deep cleansing breath as she opened the car door and slid behind the wheel, then inserting her key as she pressed the black start button.

She listened as her engine started with a roar as she raised each knee and slipped on her purple lace panties. Lacey glanced at their 7,000 square foot mansion that sat on an acre of land and wondered if it was all worth it.

Lacey knew giving up her condo to move in with Randolph was a risky move, something that he gave great resistance too, but something that Lacey insisted on. It was more of a convenience than anything since in just months she would be on her very first music tour, and paying a monthly lease on a place that sat empty just seemed senseless in her mind.

Would marrying Randolph make those feeling go away? Would this be what she needed to make her forget what happened and finally move on?

A feeling of uncertainty poured through her body and in that moment, Lacey wondered if everything would work out.

This was something she hoped and even at times prayed about it, but Lacey knew deep down inside that time would only tell, and circumstances could be a mother fucker.

# FOUR

Alex stepped out of the elevator to the lobby of her offices. It was almost 11am by the time she finally made it to work. Her mind was heavy, and she was still thinking about Malcolm and their fight earlier that morning. However, she was determined to make things good between them before the party tonight.

She sipped on her double espresso, walking with purpose through the main reception area and past her assistant, straight into her office. Without uttering a sound, she shut the door behind her and leaned against the frosted glass gathering her thoughts. She was grateful that no one remembered today was her birthday. It wasn't as if she was in the mood to celebrate - at least not right now.

Alex finally pushed herself off the door with one weary push of her butt as she headed towards her desk. On the way, she dropped her briefcase and jacket onto her chocolate leather chaise taking a few more steps before flopping her five foot eight inch frame down in her white leather chair. She glanced at the newly engraved name plate on her desk. It read *Dr. Alex Monroe, Sports Psychologist.*

Alex stared at her name plate and thought about how much she loved her job working at her alma mater UCLA. She felt fortunate to work with athletes of all different spectrums. People always seemed intrigued when she mentioned what she did for a living. It was a job that let her work with top athletes of all types to look for insight on what they needed to fix in their lives so they could improve their game.

Complex as it may sound, her job was simple. Identify what was keeping her clients from performing at their very best and what could be done to remove those mental blocks.

In turn, her clients were just like everyone else. They needed an outlet to vent about their lives and the problems that surrounded them and she was the only one who listened.

Alex loved what she did and the way it made her feel. But, for a task that came so easily in her professional life, it was somehow incredibly daunting for her personal life. *Why are other people's problems so much easier to fix than my own?* She thought as she tried to clear her mind of her misery in order to concentrate on her day.

Alex stared around her office wishing what happened between her and Malcolm had gone a different way. What she really wanted was to get to the bottom of their issues. But, she knew that the bottom was a ways away from where they stood today.

Alex closed her eyes, threw her feet up and felt the life drain out of her. She took a deep breath, tried to empty her thoughts, clear her mind, just be still.

Until the buzzer on her phone startled her, which was followed by her assistant's voice.

"Mrs. Monroe, just a reminder that you have an 11:30am appointment."

Alex felt her heart speed then slow. "Thank you, Jasmine, I'm aware of that."

Alex attempted to close her eyes, find that space of nothing, but was interrupted by her assistant a few seconds later.

"Mrs. Monroe?"

"Yes… Jasmine?"

"Do you need me to grab you anything? Coffee, tea, a croissant?"

"No, I'm fine, thanks," Alex said sounding a lot harsher than she meant. She laid her head back down and closed her eyes.

Alex slowly opened her eyes back up as she heard rustling on the other end of her phone indicating that Jasmine hadn't disconnected yet. Alex glanced back over to her phone.

"Jasmine was there something else?"

"No… well, yes… Happy Birthday, Mrs. Monroe."

Another deep breath followed by an appreciative smile, "Thank you, Jasmine."

"You're welcome."

She was never the one to make a big deal about her birthday, but the fact that Jasmine had remembered made her day a little bit better.

Alex took a few more deep breaths before attempting to close her eyes for a third time. She shifted in her seat to get comfortable, turning her head to the right when she noticed a bouquet of flowers sitting on her three-foot mahogany bookshelf near her bay window.

Alex sat up, her feet dropped to the floor and swiveled her body towards the direction of the two dozen white roses. *How did I miss those when I walked into my office*? Alex tilted her head then stood, and walked over to where they were planted. She reached out for the card, *Maybe Malcolm wasn't as mad as I thought.* She let out a short sigh of relief as she slowly opened the card to read it.

*Happy birthday to the most beautiful woman I know. XOXO*

Alex closed the card, then held it against her chest as a smile stretched across her face. She held on to the card as she walked over to where she dropped her bag; she quickly opened it as she searched inside for her cell phone. She knew Malcolm was in a meeting so she would shoot him an "I love you" text.

Alex found her phone as she slid behind her white desk and white leather chair with the high slope and lower back support, and tapped the message icon on her phone and began to type her "thank you" message to Malcolm, when her assistant buzzed her again. Alex glanced down at her Cartier Pasha diamond watch telling her she still had 20 minutes before her client arrived.

"Jasmine, I hope that isn't my client."

"No, Miss Monroe, you um… you have a visitor."

Alex put down her cell phone and pulled up her calendar on her computer and scanned it to see she didn't have anyone down. Who could be at her office other than Malcolm? But he had a meeting. In the midst of Alex trying to figure out who could be here, she heard her door open to reveal - *him.*

Alex's mouth hit the floor and bounced back up when Xavier Baker walked through her door followed by Jasmine. "Mrs. Monroe I am so sorry, but he said he wanted to surprise you and..."

Alex held a firm stare with Xavier. "It's um, it's okay Jasmine."

Jasmine noticed the immediate connection as she raised an eyebrow as a half-smile danced across her face, "Got it."

Jasmine turned, walked out the office closing the door slowly behind her.

Xavier Baker was the starting quarterback for the San Diego Chargers and the only one that made Alex sway from her marriage. Alex had not laid eyes on Xavier in over five years since their affair, as seeing him brought back too many memories, most of which she didn't want to remember.

It had been a vulnerable moment that turned into a two-month fling after Alex found a letter from a woman who claimed to be having a three-year affair with Malcolm. She'd suspected as much, but Malcolm had denied it over and over again. But, when she opened the letter addressed to her, reality flooded in.

Alex turned to Xavier to console her broken heart only to have it lead to an affair. In the moment, Alex had felt no guilt about it since most of her actions were fueled from anger and resentment. How could Malcolm do that to her? After all they had been through? After all that she thought they had together?

Malcolm swore it wasn't what she thought, and it had meant nothing to him. He promised he'd change and be a man she could love and trust, but Alex was torn. However, after thinking long and hard she decided to give Malcolm another chance to prove what he said. She loved him so very much and wanted it to work.

Alex stared at Xavier and noticed that not much had changed. He was still tall and muscular and very attractive. The years had added a more distinguished look to his dark brown complexion accompanied by his dark brown eyes, his two best attributes that always kept the women swooning.

Alex stood crossing her arms in front of her, "Well this is definitely a surprise."

"You know me, spontaneity is the spice of life," Xavier said with a wink.

As Xavier walked her way, Alex met him half way and wrapped her arms around his six foot three frame. He looked great and his 225 pounds of muscle felt even better.

"What are you doing in LA?"

"Up for a day trip. A little bit of business," Xavier scanned Alex's body from head to toe then back up to her face, "A little bit of pleasure."

Alex hung on Xavier's last words as a warm sensation swished through her body. Xavier was everything and nothing you wanted from a man, but mostly he was (and still could possibly be) Alex's weakness. The thought of him consumed her day and night after she broke it off with him and she wondered if she did the right thing, and made the right choice. Now, as he stood in front of her she wasn't so sure. Alex shifted from side to side as she made her way back over to her desk.

"That's nice, but... I'm married."

"You were married then."

Alex smiled a wide smile, Xavier had a point, but she remained firm, "I'm happily married."

Xavier's left eyebrow raised two inches before dropping back down into place, "Is that right? So Spike Lee is doing the right thing I see."

Alex let out a chuckle this time; she always loved his humor, "Yes, *he* is," Alex said, hoping she wouldn't regret her statement later.

"Well I'm happy to hear that, I really am." Xavier scanned her body once again as he licked his full lips. "You lookin' good girl, lookin' real good."

Alex took a deep breath, felt her breathing become a bit more rapid. "I'm trying to keep it together, ya know. One day at a time."

"I hear you. Well if you ever need to… *talk*, I'm here."

"That's... good to know," Alex said with a smile.

Alex walked back around her desk and sat down, "I better get back to work. I have a client in fifteen minutes."

"Right, of course, brings back memories of our… sessions." Xavier smiled as he ran his hand over his perfectly manicured goatee.

Alex took a deep breath and squeezed her legs tightly together, "I appreciate you stopping by."

"Of course," Xavier's eyes trailed behind Alex as a smile engulfed his smooth dark chocolate face, "Enjoy the flowers."

Alex's mouth fell open as her lips parted, "What?" her head whipped around to the flowers then back at Xavier, "*You* sent the flowers?"

"23 white roses and one red, I never forget what a woman loves."

Alex felt a surge of grave disappointment sail through her body, mixed with a dose of rage and a splash of embarrassment. She couldn't formulate what she wanted to say next, nor did she want too.

"Like I said, if you ever need to… *talk,*" Xavier gave Alex one last look and a smile before heading out the door.

Alex picked up her cell phone and glanced at the message that she had not sent to Malcolm, and gritted her teeth before erasing what she was going to send as a thank you. She threw her phone back down on her desk and shook her head, as she stared at the flowers her ex-lover remembered to send on her birthday.

# FIVE

Lance Monroe leaned back on the metal chair as his head fell against the concrete wall. The coldness from the wall felt good against his scalp. He slowly turned his head to the right, then left, as he scanned the holding cell where he sat trying to remember the full events of what went down the previous night that landed him in his current, unfavorable, situation - jail, specifically the downtown LA division. A sharp pain sliced through his right side as he leaned forward and grabbed it with his left hand hoping that would alleviate the discomfort.

He looked up and glanced over at the exposed commode positioned in the right corner of his four-by-eight cell and could only imagine whose ass had been on that thing. He wasn't going out like that, not in this lifetime.

"Lance Monroe?" a voice echoed down the bare hallway.

Lance straightened up his body as another sharp pain shot through his left side as he looked up to see a short and very frail police officer staring his way.

"That's me."

"You're free to go, superstar," the guard said as he unlocked his cell as Lance stood only to wince from the mounting pain in his abdomen as well as lower back. Lance shook off the pain and followed the officer down the hall and through a metal door. Lance headed into the lobby and stood in front of three guards as they each gave him one last pat down.

The tallest of the three officers then escorted Lance to a front desk, where he turned and looked at him, "I'm a big fan."

"Thanks, I appreciate that."

"I mean, regardless of your current situation."

"Cool. Good to know this didn't affect my career."

"Oh it will, just wait until those women groups gets ahold of it, I hope you have a good publicist."

"Great, thanks."

"But I'm still a fan. Hey do you mind if I get your autograph…?" He paused looking uncertain, "It's… for my son."

Lance was used to people asking for autographs, although there was a time and place for everything.

"Sure, why not?"

The officer pulled out a piece of paper and a pen and handed it to Lance. He signed his name across with his signature flourish.

The guard smiled with added excitement, "Thanks.... my son is gonna love this."

Lance nodded his head as he walked over to gather his belongings that were taken during the booking process. As he gathered his things, he continued to try and recall what actually went down last night as moments periodically flashed before him. Another blackout moment, which was not a good thing.

Lance Monroe was one of the good guys. Not perfect, but close. The kind of guy who would open the door for a woman and compliment her on her outfit. Although he wasn't raised that way, he learned fast how to win the respect of a woman and with great respect came unlimited possibilities.

A natural when it came to athletics, Lance followed his dream of one day becoming one of the greatest running backs that ever walked on an NFL field and that's exactly what he was. After graduating from UCLA, Lance was not only a first round draft pick, he signed such a lucrative contract that his signing bonus might have funded a small village in Africa.

Lance found out quickly that money and fame didn't necessarily bring happiness or love. For a moment, he did think he found both after meeting Sylvia, but unfortunately his immature ways and an unlimited supply of groupies sent him on a detour that eventually cost him the one thing he wanted most - his marriage.

Lance stepped to the counter and claimed the last of his belongings at the front desk only to turn to see Sylvia heading his way. His lips parted as a smile cascaded over his tired face. After five years of dating and three months of marriage, she still did it for him. Sylvia was definitely a sight for sore eyes, or for any eyes in his case.

He loved to watch her walk, the way her hips swayed from side to side and her left arm swung to its own up-tempo beat. Her five foot six, full body frame possessed so much purpose in each step she took, something that (in his opinion) could not be taught, and Sylvia Batista had it in spades.

Sylvia approached Lance coming just inches from his face.

"Is it me or do you get more praiseworthy every time I see you?" he asked with a grin.

Sylvia slapped a white piece of paper against Lance's chest as he reached to grab it, "Your bail has already been posted so you can save the song and dance for your groupies. That's your papers to show that you are a free man."

"Thanks. I'll pay you back."

"I pulled the money from your account. You might want to change your pin number seeing we will be divorced soon. By the way, I still haven't received your signed copies of the divorce papers yet."

Lance looked up and then back down at Sylvia, stroked the side of his face that sported a five o'clock shadow, "right, about that—"

"No more excuses Lance, you have been sitting on those papers for three weeks now, when are you going to finally sign them?"

"Well if you haven't noticed I've been a little busy lately."

"Popping bottles doesn't count."

"They do if they cost over a grand." Lance gave Sylvia a playful smile.

"I'm done playing games, have them to me by this week," Sylvia said giving Lance a more than serious look, "please."

"Fine, your wish is my command."

Sylvia then looked into her oversized khaki green leather tote and pulled out a clean shirt throwing it towards Lance.

"What's this?" he asked.

"I figured you'd need it and I was right. You smell like an orangutan dipped in Hennessy."

Lance lifted the top of his black buttoned up shirt to his nose, then winced, "Thanks."

He proceeded to pull off his shirt revealing a body that looked as if it had been photo shopped, then enhanced.

Sylvia looked away, not wanting to get sucked into his sexual portal… she was here on business, period.

"So here is the deal. I'll work your case to spin this, for double what I usually charge. You don't ask any questions, and you do what I say."

Pulling out a vanilla folder, Sylvia didn't miss a beat, while Lance listened to her, bemused.

"Now I did a little digging and found out that the woman you were with has priors, one being bad check writing, so we can definitely spin this as her being the aggressor. We can make this look like she was after your money. Until everything clears, it'd probably be in your best interest to lay low for a while until this blows over. No partying, no strip clubs, no Vegas trips. You go to work, you come home and you are definitely in bed by 10."

"Are you serious?"

Sylvia stopped and looked at Lance directly in the eye. She folded and closed the folder she was holding.

"Nope, actually, I'm trying out my new stand up material on you. Apparently you don't realize the multitude of shit you're in for and it's about time you learned you need to grow the fuck up."

"Whoa, whoa, whoa." Lance's body wrenched back as a huge sarcastic smile traveled across his face. Now this was the Sylvia he loved. "Where is this malevolence coming from? Last time I checked, we were separated."

"Yeah, well the last time I checked you were a liar and a cheater who couldn't honor a commitment."

Unable to control his laughter, a chuckle escaped before he could throw on a semi-serious expression. "This profusion of venom spewing from your lips is well… inadmissible."

Sylvia looked at Lance like she had just bitten into a ripe lemon, "You know, for someone who uses such big words, your action speaks volumes of your vapid ignorance."

Lance's small smirk on his face quickly blossomed into a full-fledged smile; he was loving this moment. "Vapid ignorance. I like your choice of wording. I may have to add that to my vernacular."

Sylvia rolled her eyes, feeling them knocking against the back of her head, "Please stop."

"Hey they didn't nickname me 'The Professor' on the field because I was known to sport a bow tie from time to time on my off days. I brought the knowledge, don't you forget that."

"Can I please continue?" she asked, clearly done with his attitude.

"Of course."

"So what really happened last night? And since I'm just your publicist and soon to be ex-wife you can actually tell me the truth this time."

Lance shook his head as a serious tone overtook him, "I honestly don't remember," he said sadly.

Silence fell between them, and Sylvia felt a sadness take over her for she knew what he was going through.

"You're blackouts are getting worse, aren't they?"

Lance looked away; his silence spoke volumes.

Sylvia sighed, "Lance you really need to stop drinking."

Lance stood there contemplating what Sylvia was saying but in reality it was the drinking that was the only thing that got him through the night.

"Hey if I needed someone to psychoanalyze me I would go see a shrink," he shot back.

"That's something I've been saying to you for years, this is nothing new and I never claimed to psychoanalyze anyone." Sylvia knew that would touch a nerve but it needed to be said.

"Listen, I don't need this right now. Are you gonna help me spin this shit or not? Yes or no?"

Sylvia shifted, locking eyes with Lance, not letting them go, "I will on one condition."

Lance threw up his arms in protest, "Screw the damn conditions, okay?"

"I'm only trying to help, I'm on your side."

"That's where you're wrong, no one is on my side." Lance turned and walked two steps, and then heard:

"I want to help you, but you can't keep running from your past," Sylvia threw out.

Lance clenched his teeth, felt the pain of the pressure as the side of his mouth pulsated. He turned walking back towards Sylvia; they were now face to face.

"Yes, or no Sylvia?"

Sylvia bit her lip, knew it wasn't that simple, knew there was so much more.

"Fine, I will take that as a no. Thanks for bailing me out. I'm going home."

Lance started walking away from Sylvia.

"And how do you expect to get there?" Sylvia threw his way.

He stopped, still angry, slowly turning back towards her, "I guess I'll just take the fucking bus."

Sylvia shook her head, a groan escaped from her parted lips, "Yeah, good luck with that."

Without so much as a response, Lance turned towards the exit of the police station and strutted towards the door, punching it open as he walked outside. As the metal door closed behind him, he knew Sylvia was right; he also knew how much he had hurt her, unfortunately, he knew he didn't come close to deserving her.

# SIX

"The last thing I needed was that shit from Alex this morning. Not today, not when I was about to walk into one of the most important meetings of my life," Malcolm said out loud stepping out of the elevator on the fifth floor of Paramount Pictures.

He walked towards suite 515 and caught a glance of his reflection staring back through the glass double doors. Malcolm stopped, looked and surveyed his gear, a brown suede jacket over a white t-shirt complemented his faded jeans and camel colored Gucci suede shoes. *I gotta keep it casual, I'm a filmmaker, not a corporate guy,* Malcolm thought to himself as he pushed through the glass doors and strutted up to the receptionist with much confidence.

He never knew what to expect when walking into these types of meetings, but what he knew for sure was that he had a movie that needed distribution and was there to get it, period.

"Hi can I help you?" The young and attractive receptionist looked up at Malcolm and smiled with her best *Welcome to Hollywood* smile.

"Malcolm Monroe here to see Jay Douglas. I have a 10:30 meeting with him."

"Of course, let me buzz him and tell him you are here... have a seat please."

"Thanks." Malcolm turned and took a seat in their waiting room equipped with a black leather couch, two matching chairs and a 42" flat screen TV that was playing World War Z.

Malcolm glanced up and then back down, felt his nerves getting the best of him, so he stood, walked the length of the couch, sat back down, clasped his hands together, said a small prayer to the man above before looking up to see Jay Douglas himself standing less than three feet from him.

"Jay," Malcolm said, greeting the executive. He got off the couch, extending a hand out to him. Malcolm took it, feeling the strong hand shake.

"Glad you could make it in, Malcolm, we've been looking forward to this."

"Likewise, Jay, likewise," Malcolm took a deep breath and felt his adrenaline slow, as he followed Jay back to the conference room.

Malcolm knew landing Paramount Pictures would put him back in the race; a studio of this size could guarantee his film 120 screens easily. A candid detour to the road back to the top.

The journey back to the top hadn't been easy but Malcolm was determined to not give up, that just wasn't an option in his book. Like he told Alex, "I am a filmmaker period, it is all I know and all I ever want to do. I didn't go through four years of film school to shit it away by working at an insurance company selling policies I wouldn't even buy, nope, Malcolm Monroe is on a mission to change the world, one film at a time."

Twenty minutes passed after sitting down with Jay and his two colleagues; small talk was big in Hollywood. The people who stayed were the ones who excelled at it, because the ones who weren't didn't make it past go.

"So we saw the film and we think it was tastefully done," Jay looked directly into Malcolm's eyes, then quickly to the other two colleagues sitting next to him.

Silence fell over the room and Malcolm swallowed hard. He felt a pull in his side. This wasn't good, not good at all, Malcolm thought as he felt beads of perspiration beginning to form on the back of his neck.

"I'm… I'm glad you think so, Jay," Malcolm said still waiting for that other fucking shoe to come swooping down.

"Yes, good choice of shots, a lot of directors are afraid to get up close and personal, to try and really add that dramatic feel, but not over doing it." The second guy in the room said before shooting Jay a glance then back at Malcolm.

*What the fuck was going on?* Malcolm thought. He was hating this moment, this game of come fuck me if you can.

"So you liked the film?" Malcolm finally threw out the bait, screw waiting for it.

Jay shifted in his seat, cleared his throat, "We did… it's just that… it's not what we're looking for right now."

Malcolm felt his heart drop to his shoes as his mouth dried up faster than the Mojave Desert.

"I'm sorry, come again Jay?" Malcolm sat up erect in his seat, making sure he heard him correctly.

"You see, a film like yours, of that nature."

"And what nature would that be?" Malcolm asked.

"A dramatic nature."

Malcolm rubbed his chin with his hand, "So you're saying my film is too dramatic?"

The third guy, the one who had been playing on his phone for the duration of the meeting finally spoke up, "There's death in your movie," he said without looking up.

"Excuse me."

"Death, there is death in your movie." The guy finally lifted his head, giving Malcolm eye contact for the first time.

"Okay, and that's a problem?"

"People don't want to come to the movies to be depressed."

"Correct me if I'm wrong, Jay, but didn't Paramount do not one, but three pictures this year that was about death?"

All three men shifted in their seats, shooting looks at each other like they were playing a game of catch with their uncomfortable glances.

"Yes, we did… but that was different."

"Different, how, Jay?"

As the uncomfortable glances continued to shoot around the room then picking up speed, Malcolm could feel his temperature boiling over.

"How?" Malcolm repeated himself, this time with more affliction in his voice.

"It's just different when it comes to… to… African American movies."

Malcolm fell back onto the couch as his hands slapped down onto his thighs, *you have got to be fucking kidding me*, he thought. Malcolm slowly looked back up, "Wow… well this is very, very disappointing."

"Malcolm it's just that your people…"

"My people," Malcolm nodded his head in disgust and frustration, "great."

"African Americans already have it hard enough. I think they want to see films that make them laugh, uplift them even."

"So now you're an expert on my culture? I cannot believe what I'm hearing."

"Listen, we knew this would cause a bit of an uproar, so we were prepared with a solution," Jay said.

Malcolm stopped himself in mid-speech wondering what kind of *solution* they could possibly have. "A solution, is that so?"

"Yes." Jay sat up and clasps his hands together, "If you are willing to tell the story about your father, then we would be happy to stand behind this movie one hundred percent. We're talking distribution, marketing, the whole works."

Malcolm stared at Jay, not believing what he was hearing. *Has this white boy lost his mind?*

"Jay, you just sat here and told me you didn't want death in *our* films… should I remind you that my father, the great R&B Legend is *dead* and a movie would actually show that?"

Jay smiled a condescending smile, "Well that's different, the story wouldn't harp on his death, but his life as one of the greatest artists that ever lived."

"Your dad was a legend," another one of the studio men piped up.

Malcolm stood, unable to stomach this meeting one minute longer, "This is some bullshit, you know that, right? Here I am coming to you with a quality black film with quality actors and you tell me it's 'not what you are looking for,' but oh, oh, but the life and death of my father is?"

Jay and his colleagues just stared at Malcolm, clearly what Malcolm was saying made perfect sense to them.

"Just think about it, Malcolm."

"Thank you, but no fucking thank you."

Malcolm snatched up his briefcase with all his might, turned and headed out the room, closing the door behind him. He walked with purpose back down the hallway, through the lobby, past the Hollywood receptionist and the big screen TV playing World *War Z* and out to the main hallway.

He stopped at the elevators and took a deep breath, leaning against the wall, trying to calm himself. He tried to figure out why this shit was happening to him. He hated the fact that everything… everything led back to his father. Even twenty years after his death, he couldn't escape Langston Monroe.

Malcolm shook his head and spoke candidly to himself, "At least now I know how I landed this meeting."

Malcolm's thoughts continued to stir up trouble, leading him to wonder if his initial success was only because of his dad and not from any talent he might have. He wondered if he could ever escape his father's shadow. He wondered if the world knew exactly the person his father was and if they would still care about his life, his music or his legend.

Malcolm clenched his jaws, felt the stress of his life setting up residency in his body, couldn't shake the thought of his late father, how his music blazed a trail for the continued evolution of black music everywhere. How he was known not only for his funk and jazz but his infectious personality, one that his fans and public grew to know him as, grew to love him as and grew to mourn him by, even after twenty years.

The elevator doors opened as Malcolm pulled out his cell phone and dialed a number, a familiar number.

A female voice on the other end, gave him some solace. Malcolm hit the button that flashed lobby as the elevator doors closed.

"Hey, it's Malcolm, I need to see you."

# SEVEN

Lacey needed to calm her nerves before she walked into a meeting with her newly signed record label, Roland Records.

She noticed a Starbucks just down the street from where her meeting was scheduled as she turned down 4th avenue in Santa Monica. Lacey quickly parked her car in the parking structure and took her long strides down 4th Ave and over to Colorado Blvd. The sun felt good as it rested on her light brown sienna skin.

She entered Starbucks and felt a sudden surge of annoyance ricochet through her body at the sight of the long line.

*What is it about this coffee that people cannot get enough of?* Lacey thought as she moved toward the front of the counter ignoring the five-person line as if she were the only customer in the store.

"Hi, I'm gonna need a double shot of espresso."

The twenty something cashier gave Lacey a timid look, "Um Miss, there is a line..." he said in his most hesitant, *I'm still not used to rude customers*, tone.

Lacey raised an annoyed eyebrow, "I see that, but I'm in a hurry and I cannot afford to wait, not today."

"I understand but..."

"Fine. How about I just pay for everyone's coffee in line? Is that better? Now please, can you just ring me up for a double shot of espresso? Thank you." Lacey slapped two twenty dollar bills on the counter, looking back at the patrons she rudely skipped over as they all stared her way.

"You're welcome," she shot them all a pompous glare.

She took four steps and moved to the opposite end of the counter, folding her arms and tapping her foot on the tri-colored tile while awaiting her double shot of espresso.

Now all eyes in the coffee shop were on Lacey. She didn't mind, she was used to it and even loved getting a dose of it.

As Lacey stood there glaring down at her gold Rolex watch in five-second intervals she noticed a woman standing a few feet away from her. Her blue and white pinstriped suit with matching clutch immediately caught Lacey's attention; she was always drawn to style and this woman definitely had a lot of it.

Lacey threw the woman an informal smile before glancing back over at the small cluster of Starbucks workers wondering if they had to go to Columbia to get the stupid beans to create her double shot of espresso. She needed her caffeine yesterday.

Lacey looked up only to notice the woman staring her way once again. She wondered if she knew this woman from somewhere. She wondered if the woman knew her.

Lacey threw out yet another informal smile as she slowly glanced behind her wondering if she was indeed the intended target. Upon noticing the man in a dark grey tailored suit with a black t-shirt underneath behind her, it was now clear that he was this woman's intended target, not *her*. Lacey cut her eyes away from the guy as she stepped out of the line of the two's irksome eye play.

Lacey sighed and folded her arms as she redirected her attention back to the Starbucks workers, giving them an "I can't wait all day" look. The worker behind the counter sped up her coffee making as Lacey turned to notice the woman in the pinstriped suit was now standing just inches away from her, awaiting her coffee along with everyone else. Now sandwiched between him and her and their annoying glances, Lacey took one step back giving them both the center stage.

The woman acknowledged Lacey's gesture as she turned and gave her a knowing smile, then slowly turned her head straight again, but still directing her statement to Lacey, "That was quite a show you put on earlier."

The woman's statement prompted Lacey to look over at the woman who was now staring directly at her.

"I'm sorry are you talking to me?"

"Yep, sure am."

A sarcastic grin spread across Lacey's face as she rolled her eyes up in her head before dropping them back down to focus on her intended target, "Yeah, well, I'm late for a very important meeting."

A small chuckle escaped from the woman's mouth.

Lacey did a micro swivel on her right heel to face the woman with the pinstripe suit, "Is there something funny about that?"

"Have you ever heard the saying, 'Lack of preparation on your part does not necessitate an emergency on my part?'"

The man in the dark grey suit with the black t-shirt raised an eyebrow as he threw out a devious smile before walking up to the counter, grabbing his coffee and heading out the door.

Lacey redirected her attention back to the woman standing next to her, "Did you just look that up this morning?"

The woman turned her body towards Lacey and they were now in a deadlock stare, "I'm sure I speak for *everyone* standing here this morning, we are *all* in a hurry."

They continued to stare at each other before Lacey broke the silence, "You got a free cup of coffee out of it, be grateful for that." Lacey cut her eyes away from the woman as she stepped up to the counter and grabbed her double shot of espresso off the brown and white speckled countertop with one continuous swipe.

"You have a good day." With that, Lacey turned on her right foot and headed out the cafe. She looked back to see a smirk on the woman's face before heading to her meeting.

Ten minutes later after getting her coffee fix for the day, Lacey felt a calmness as she rode the glass elevator up to the 11th floor. She hummed along to the soft melody of Alicia Keys floating through the air and a small smile broke through on her preoccupied face as it quickly blossomed at the thought of her emerging career as a singer. A moment that Lacey had been waiting for, for years.

As a child Lacey loved watching her father rehearse in the studio and knew one day she'd be standing on a stage of her own with millions of fans cheering her name. Lacey loved the spotlight and let her mind drift back to a warm day in July when she snuck into her father's studio to listen to him rehearse…A lot of things back then didn't make sense at the time, but they still stuck out in her mind.

*A five-year-old Lacey sat quietly outside her father's small studio in their west wing of the home listening to him sing a new song. Usually Lacey preferred to play with her Barbie dolls, but today, something about this song drew her down to his studio. She loved the sound of her daddy's voice. It was so strong and soothing and it made her want to do what he did.*

*Lacey peered around the corner of the open door to catch a peek of her dad singing as he played along on his keyboard. Stopping and starting as he would write a note down on his notebook. Lacey caught her father looking her way as she quickly sat back, hoping that he didn't see her. She knew he didn't like to be interrupted when he was in his music room, so she tried to keep as quiet as possible.*

*"I see you over there baby girl," Langston Monroe said as the music stopped. Lacey peered back around the corner only this time to be greeted with a warm smile from her father.*

*"Come on in here."*

*Lacey stood with much apprehension and slowly walked towards her father. He was a handsome man, jet black curly hair with a smooth butterscotch complexion. His studio always smelled of tobacco which was evident of a chain smoker. Today was no different as she glanced at the ashtray that sat on top of his piano filled with small buds and one lit cigarette. The one thing Lacey remembered most about her father was that he always smelled like cigarettes mixed with a sharp musk sent.*

*"Is that a new song?"*

*"Yes it is. It's gonna be a hit too. You like it?"*

*Lacey slowly nodded her head yes.*

*"What do you like about it?"*

*"When I heard it, it made me feel happy."*

*"Well that's what it was supposed to do. I like to write music that uplifts people and puts a smile on their face."*

*"Why is that?"*

*"Because there are too many sad people in the world right now."*

*"Will it make Mama feel happy? Will it make her stop crying so much?"*

*Langston looked at Lacey, the one question he could not answer. It was the one thing he couldn't explain to his five-year-old daughter. The one thing he chose not to.*

*"Listen, why don't you go play outside with your brother."*

*"I don't want to he's playing stupid basketball. I hate basketball, I want to stay here with you."*

*"Daddy needs to work, so go on."*

*Lacey was quiet, then looked at her dad, "Are you going to be home tonight to read me a story?"*

*"Not tonight, baby, maybe tomorrow."*

*"But you said that yesterday," Lacey said, dropping her head. Langston took a deep breath as he placed his hand on the side of her face, sliding it down to her chin then lifting her head, their eyes met.*

*"I'll try, but Daddy is a very busy man. I have to keep writing these songs so you can live in this big beautiful house and dress up in all your pretty dresses, okay?"*

*Lacey sat quietly and just stared back at the floor. She really could care less about their big fancy house and beautiful dresses, she just wanted her father around more than what he was and she needed to tell him that.*

*"Daddy..."*

*Lacey heard a phone ring. Langston walked over to the phone sitting on a table across the room. He picked up the phone as his voice dropped to a low tone. Lacey stood still as she tried her best to hear what her father was saying.*

*Langston laughed into the phone before turning to his daughter to see that he was her main attraction, "I'll see you in a few minutes," he said before placing the phone back down, then he glanced Lacey's way. "I have to go baby girl."*

*He walked back over to Lacey, put out his cigarette and grabbed his jacket. "I'll try my best to be back to read you a story."*

*Before Lacey had a chance, Langston kissed her on the forehead and headed out the room. She heard the sound of his footsteps fade away only to totally disappear completely. Lacey stared around his studio, breathed in the smell of stale cigarettes and felt a sense of resentment to the person on the phone who'd just stolen her time away.*

As the elevator doors opened at the 11th floor, Lacey stepped into the lobby of Roland Records to the eager eyes of her agent Drew Thomas. "Why are you late?"

"I needed coffee, is that such a crime?"

"It's a huge crime when we're meeting with the president of your new label."

"If I recall, it was them who came after me, not the other way around."

Drew took a deep breath, he had to remind himself that dealing with divas is just par for the course in his business. In his mind, it was the only downside to his exciting career as a music agent/producer.

Drew Thomas was an up and coming agent and determined to make a name for himself in this industry. Drew was a typical fast-talking, deal-making agent and his biggest strength was that he didn't take no for an answer.

"I understand, but what you have to remember is in order to break the rules you have to play by them first."

"Ah, is that how this business works?" Lacey said in her sarcastic tone, knowing good and well how this business worked. However, Lacey was never one to follow any rules and she wasn't about to start now.

"Let's not get dropped before our first tour, okay? I worked too hard to get you here."

"Well, I am the daughter of Langston Monroe."

"I understand, but remember, we are making a name for you, not following in your father's shadow. It's about Lacey Monroe, not the daughter of Langston Monroe. I'm your agent and I've gotten you this far. Don't steal the wheel from me now."

Lacey took an annoyed breath, "Fine, steer away if you must."

"Thank you. Now let's go in here and work out this tour schedule. This is it. Your time to shine! You ready?"

"I was born ready," Lacey said as she flipped her shoulder length hair.

"Great, they're waiting for us."

The two headed down the hall lined with framed records and smiling photos of other artists big and small to a large corner office with large windows. Upon entering Lacey scanned the name on the door, Doug Roland, CEO of Roland record label. Lacey threw on her *I am a star* smile as she headed through the door.

Drew made the announcement as Lacey walked in, "I would like to introduce to you your new rising star, the lovely and extremely talented, Lacey Monroe!"

Lacey beamed from ear to ear from the introduction as she sauntered into the office only to have her enthusiasm cut short by a site that took her breath away. Sitting on the couch next to the CEO of Roland Records was *her*, the woman in the blue pinstriped suit and amazing body staring back her way. *What the hell is she doing here?* Lacey thought to herself while trying to keep a casual smile on her face.

"Lacey I would like you to meet Doug Roland CEO and Jana Taylor, your tour manager."

*Tour manager?* Lacey thought as her right eye brow shot up to her neatly cut bangs. *This has to be a joke.*

Jana stood and extended her hand towards Lacey. "We meet again."

Lacey, wasn't really sure how to feel about the woman she just got into it with, being her tour manager.

"Yes, we do," Lacey said as she reluctantly slid her hand into Jana's only to have their eyes connect once again.

"You two know each other?" Drew blurted out with a grin on his face.

"Yes, we go way back… twenty minutes ago down at Starbucks," Jana said, looking Drew's way then quickly back at Lacey. Lacey shook her head as she stared Jana's way noticing her short tomboy hair cut that framed her oval face and strong features. Her pinstriped jacket was neatly buttoned around her small waist, showing off her hourglass figure, and round rear end, a body that screamed "I work out five days a week and most weekends." *Whatever.* Lacey knew she was hating but that's what she was good at doing.

Lacey's enthusiastic agent interjected breaking Lacey's train of thought, "Gotta love Starbucks."

"For sure. Let's get to business shall we?" Jana said taking a seat in the black leather chair crossing her right leg over her left as she unbuttoned the one large button on her jacket, revealing a fitted white tank. The sight of Jana's fitted white top drew Lacey's eyes to Jana's chest, then up to her face, then quickly away.

Jana let out a half smirk until switching back into business mode, "So of course you know we are here concerning Lacey's upcoming tour that is scheduled to start in 4 months."

Jana shot a quick look at Lacey and back at Drew, and then pulled out a folder and placed it on the table. "I have a list of cities we have on her tour list."

"And how many would that be?" Drew asked, before even surveying the list that Jana had provided him.

Jana uncrossed her legs, "Well, we are looking at the main markets right now, New York, Atlanta, Chicago and of course right here in LA."

"Wow, that's not a lot of cities," Drew chimed in again as he scooped up the list from the table that divided them.

"We are a relatively small label and we need to be careful not to blow out our overhead, if you know what I mean," Doug intervened. The CEO was a man of very few words, so when he did speak, he made sure they counted.

"Understandable, Mr. Roland," Drew intervened, "but we aren't dealing with a new comer to the game, this is the lovely Lacey Monroe extraordinaire!"

Jana smiled as she looked at Doug then back at Drew, "Lacey is already signed to the label, until she sells some albums in retrospect, she is a new comer," Jana shot Lacey another look.

"She's got a great twitter following, that alone should justify adding a few more cities," Drew continued, sitting on the edge of his seat. He wasn't about to give up on what he was there to accomplish – more tour cities.

"We don't want to over assume ticket sales, now do we?" Doug said in a firm tone before hearing his cell phone ring. He looked at the display, "Excuse me I have to take this," he stood and walked out of the office.

Drew didn't miss a beat as he continued to negotiate, not quite yet letting go of the additional cities. "Okay, let's look at the numbers here, in one week Lacey's twitter following jumped from 500 to 500,000. You can't tell me that's not worth adding three more markets to the tour."

"Right, but that was only once people found out that she was the daughter of legendary singer Langston Monroe. Loved your father by the way."

Lacey gave Jana a slight smile with a tilt of her head, but no verbal acknowledgment.

"Lacey still needs to get out there and earn those fans through her vocals and performance."

"And she will," Drew shot back.

"I'm confident that she will," Jana concurs with Drew.

"I have a question," Lacey interjected in between refreshing her lip gloss.

"Sure?" Jana said looking her way.

"What experience do *you* have? Assuming you will be the tour manager," Lacey's question threw an unexpected chill swirling throughout the room. Jana looked at Drew as Drew looked at Jana then Lacey, as the awkward silence fell between all parties involved.

Jana finally revealed a vexed smile. "I am the tour manager," she said in a slow matter of fact tone.

"I see…" Lacey just stared at Jana and waited for her to answer her initial question.

Jana took a deep breath and a sarcastic grin unrolled across her face. She'd dealt with singers far worse than Lacey, that's for sure.

"I have over 15 years of tour management experience working with artists such as Maxwell, The Roots and Jill Scott."

Lacey sat back in her chair, crossed her arms, "Well Jill Scott is a good friend of mine, I'll give her a call and ask what she thought of you."

"Why don't you do that, in the meantime can we get back to business at hand?"

Lacey looked away and nonchalantly started to text on her phone, ignoring Jana's last statement.

Jana kept her professional demeanor; it was obvious that Lacey did not scare nor intimidate her, not one bit. Jana directed her attention to Drew.

"Drew, let me be blunt here, these next few months are a testing ground for Lacey. And Lacey..." Lacey looked up at Jana, "I have no doubt that you will get out there and be the next fucking Beyoncé, but let's not bite off more than we can chew, okay?"

Lacey looked back down at her phone.

"So that said, we are settled on the four main markets and already have some great venues locked down." Jana waited for Drew's confirmation.

"Sounds good, Jana," Drew said, still a little put off with Lacey's lack of professionalism.

"We are on the same team Drew, let's not forget that."

Drew nodded his head slowly, "That we are."

"Great, let's sign the paperwork for the tour then."

As Drew pulled out the paper work, Lacey and Jana stared at each other before Jana redirected her attention back to Drew.

Twenty minutes and several signatures later, Lacey and Drew were wrapped up in last minute talks in the lobby following their meeting when Lacey noticed Jana headed their way. Lacey turned her attention back to her agent only to notice that Jana had stopped just short of them.

"Lacey, hey, you got a minute?" Jana called over to her.

Lacey gave Drew a look.

"Go ahead I have to get to my next meeting. Nice to finally meet you Jana, I look forward to our prosperous adventure together."

"Likewise."

"Lacey, I will call you later," Drew said before planting a small kiss on Lacey's cheek and jumping on the elevator.

As the doors of the elevator closed, Jana turned her attention solely to Lacey, "Well I'm glad one of you is excited about working with me," Jana said with a smile.

"Why would you say that, Jana?"

Jana laughed as she looked down then back up, "Okay listen, I think we got off on the wrong foot."

"We?"

"Yes, *we.* Listen, we have a lot to pull together in the next 4 months, I just want to make sure from here on out we can agree to be civil to each other for the sake of the tour and your career."

"I think my career will be fine. I think it's yours you ought to be worried about. Tour managers are extremely replaceable."

Jana chuckled again, "Okay, Lacey I…"

"You can call me Ms. Monroe," Lacey quickly corrected Jana with a straight face. They held a stare as Lacey noticed a small crease beginning to form in the middle of Jana's forehead.

"I really don't think you are in a position to be throwing out threats." Jana's tone was serious, very serious.

"Well I disagree," Lacey shot back on the heels of Jana's last word.

Jana smiled a broad, controlled, smile, took a small step towards Lacey and dropped her voice down a few octaves. Her eyes darkened and narrowed, "You might want to be careful of who you step on, on the way up. It just might be the ass that you're kissing on the way down." Jana took two steps back, "Have a good one."

Lacey watched as Jana glided down the hallway, disappearing into the far right office. There was something that felt familiar about her, something she couldn't put her finger on... yet.

# EIGHT

"I just got off the phone with the president of the San Francisco 49ers… A position opened up for head psychology and I am recommending you for the position."

Alex just stared at her boss, Dr. Blackwell, as he stood in the doorway of her office awaiting a reaction to the news he just dropped onto her. It was two-thirty and Alex was packing up to leave for the day.

"Come again?" Alex shot back, making sure she heard what she thought she had heard correctly.

Dan Blackwell slowly shut the door behind him as he walked over to her desk, taking a seat in the chair positioned in front of it. "Apparently their head of sports psychiatry accepted a job with the Cowboys and they're looking for a replacement."

"The season has already started?" Alex said"

"Well, that is why they are looking to replace ASAP."

Dr. Blackwell crossed his legs, smoothed out his burgundy tie with silver diamonds and smiled as his eyes shot back up to Alex, still frozen in the same spot.

Alex felt a tightness in her stomach as if someone was pushing the inner lining together. "I'm speechless."

"I know, it's a lot to take in but I wanted to give you a heads up before you left for the weekend, you know, time to think it over, discuss with your husband."

"Well thank you, although, now probably isn't the best time for me to be relocating," Alex said as she had a flash back of the morning's argument with Malcolm.

"Why is that?" Dan looked curious as to her reasons. "If I may pry."

Alex dropped her shoulders as her body fell down into her office chair, "Well most of what Malcolm does is here in LA… and…" Alex stopped herself, trying not to reveal too much of her inner thought, inner turmoil, her inner personal drama that should stay just that, personal. She wasn't in therapy after all.

"He's a filmmaker correct?"

"That he is," Alex said as she noticed Dan's eyes shoot left then right, an indication of a mind in action.

"So he can shoot a film anywhere, right?"

Alex chuckled at Dan's logic since she felt the same way, but of course, that was logic she had to keep buried beneath her verbal say.

"Technically, yes, but unfortunately Malcolm thinks he needs to be here in LA."

Dan looked at Alex then down at his tie, contemplating his next thought, his persuasive wording, "Well I don't want to rock any boats in your household, but this could be a golden opportunity for you if they decide to go your way."

"I understand that," Alex said feeling the butterflies churning up the pit of her stomach. This should be the best news of her life, but instead it felt like a tease. She loved Malcolm, but at times like these, she resented having to rely on his say so in a decision such as her career and her life.

"You know you'll be looking at doubling your salary along with having full benefits, access to the owner's jet, expense account and signing bonus."

Alex who was sitting on the edge of her seat dropped her five foot eight frame back into her white leather chair, "You're not making this easy to turn down. By the way, I'm honored that you even considered me for the position."

Dan's eyebrows pressed together causing two creases to appear in his forehead, "Are you kidding me? You are one of my best psychiatrists here and to be honest, I think you would be a great fit for their organization."

"Thank you, Dan, I truly appreciate that." Alex didn't know what to think other than she felt even more torn than a few minutes ago. Alex began to weigh the pros and cons in her head like running credits at the end of a movie.

"Of course I won't be happy to lose you but you can't stay on the college level forever. It's time to move up."

Alex's mind continued to tick as she fluffed her hair with her fingers. Dan was right, she had to start thinking about transitioning to professional teams and this was what she'd been working for all these years.

Though, now that the day had finally come, it couldn't have come at a worse time. But in all fairness, Malcolm didn't technically have to reside in LA. Maybe Alex was jumping the gun to assume that Malcolm would be totally against moving. Maybe he would welcome the change.

"What kind of timeframe are we on here Dan?"

"Well if all goes smoothly I would like to have you on a flight up to the Bay area next week for interviews. A decision should be made within a week after that."

"Wow, that's pretty fast."

"As I mentioned, they're looking to replace the position ASAP."

"Apparently."

Dan stood, brushed his slacks as if he was knocking off lint, "But we can talk more about it tonight at your birthday party; I don't want to hold you up here, you must have a lot to prepare for. My wife is looking forward to catching up with you."

"Same here."

"Well, I will see you later tonight, and think about it Alex. This will be a great fit for you."

Dan turned and headed for the door when Alex heard something come out of her mouth that she couldn't pull back, nor in the moment did she wanted to, "Actually Dan, go ahead and set up the interview."

Dan stopped and turned back towards Alex, a surprised look illuminated on his face, "You sure? You don't want to discuss it with Malcolm, first?"

"I will. I don't want to wait until Monday to let you know. This job sounds like what I have been waiting for a long time. I'd like to get the ball rolling."

Dan shook his head vigorously up and down, "Okay then… I will give him a call back today."

Alex took a deep breath, "Great." She felt her emotions begin to wrestle for supremacy. She couldn't decide if she were excited or scared.

"And happy birthday, Alex. You don't look a day older than when we met."

That compliment brought a huge smile to Alex's face as Dan closed the door behind him.

Alex sat up again on her seat. She wasn't exactly sure how Malcolm would react to a move, but what she did know was this was the best thing for her career right now and maybe it was time to start thinking about herself for a change.

Alex's mind continued to contemplate the job, how San Francisco was only a 50-minute flight and many couples have survived a long distance relationship for a period of time. It was time she started putting herself first and stop tiptoeing around Malcolm's feelings with his career.

Alex leaned over and picked up her cell phone, as she scrolled for Malcolm's number, she tapped his name as she listened to it ring a few times before going into voicemail. She hung up, taking a deep breath. She could discuss it with him when she got home, before the party.

Alex had a good feeling about this. She had a good feeling about everything. Things were about to take a major turn and she was ready for whatever came her way, she hoped.

# NINE

"Wow, you definitely need to have more bad meetings more often… that was a-mazing." Nikki Bryant gazed at Malcolm as they both lay in her bed enjoying the afterglow of their love making.

Malcolm sat silent as Nikki reached over, grabbed a cigarette and lit it up. She took a long drag before exhaling and passing it over to Malcolm who quickly took it from her and inhaled.

He sat up leaning against the bare cold white wall and took one more drag before handing the cigarette back to Nikki. His head dropped towards Nikki and his eyes scanned her butterscotch toned body and silky smooth skin. He admired how her reddish complexion matched the brown swirls in her carpet that covered her 400 square foot studio apartment.

Nikki was the perfect mix of a Puerto Rican mother and African American father. A gorgeous combination created from a perfect alignment of the stars. There was no doubt that Nikki was beyond beautiful, a trait that drew Malcolm to her immediately. There was also no doubt that she was in love with Malcolm and was willing to do anything for him. Something that Malcolm knew and used to his advantage.

Malcolm turned his head away from Nikki as he glanced around her scarcely furnished studio which consisted of a bed with no frame, a tube TV, sheets for curtains and clothes scattered all over the floor. At 25, Nikki was the poster child for a starving artist.

"When are you going to get some furniture?"

"Why would I get furniture when we are moving in together soon?" Nikki said.

Malcolm looked away as Nikki sat up at attention. "We are getting a place together, right?"

Malcolm continued to look away before turning his head back in her direction, "I never said that, Nik." Malcolm reached over and grabbed another cigarette. He hated that he started smoking again, he had been doing so well until he met Nikki. A habit he picked up on the set of his first film. He hated that smoking calmed him and lately he needed a lot of self-soothing.

"I guess that was orgasmic talk, I get it. Maybe I should go out and get a second man, it would only be fair, don't you think?"

"Nikki, slow down. I told you it's not that easy. I'm married and..."

"I know, I know. But eventually you're going to have to deliver on all these promises you're throwing my way. Don't take me for granted, Malcolm, I'm a fucking catch."

Malcolm looked away, took a pull of his cigarette, "Is that a threat?"

Nikki just stared at Malcolm, he knew she would never leave; what she didn't know was that he wouldn't let her.

"I have to pee." Nikki jumped off the bed and walked stark naked into the bathroom, shutting the door behind her.

Malcolm rubbed his head and took a deep breath as he thought about what Nikki was saying. With everything going on in his life, he'd forgotten his comment about them getting a place together.

But that was months ago and for Malcolm, every day brought something different that he had to make a decision about. Although the decision to end it with Nikki never crossed his mind, why would he?

He knew he was treading on thin ice with Nikki and making promises he wasn't sure he could deliver. In his mind he really didn't know what he wanted. But at the same time, in his mind he really wanted it all.

Malcolm's mind drifted as to why he even started the affair with Nikki eight months ago, how she made him feel like a big time director while he was struggling to regain his name back. Nikki looked up to him, admired him, and most importantly, stroked his bruised ego. A task that Nikki did with ease, Alex found difficult to achieve. Malcolm thought back to when he first laid eyes on Nikki.

He *was writing at Michelle's Cafe not too far from his house in Sherman Oaks when he heard a female voice directing a question his way.*

*"Are you done with that?"*

*Malcolm looked up from his laptop to see the owner of the voice hovering over him.*

*"Excuse me?"*

*"You're coffee, are you done?"*

*Malcolm had never seen her before out of the three years he had been writing there and well, he was definitely intrigued.*

*"I um… I am," Malcolm said, clearly captivated by her beauty.*

*"Can I get you another?" she said as she tilted her head and smiled almost simultaneously on cue.*

*"Definitely, you must have been reading my mind," Malcolm said, continuing to hold the gaze of the very attractive woman with sandy brown hair and hazel eyes.*

*"You're new here. I can say that because I've been coming to this cafe for the last three years and I've never seen you before."*

*"I am. I'm Nikki."*

*"Nice to meet you… I'm Malcolm..."*

*"Monroe, I know," Nikki quickly blurted out then blushed.*

*Malcolm sat back, crossing his arms over his chest, "Have we met?"*

*"No, but I follow your work, well actually, I read an interview with you in Write ON Magazine a few months back."*

*Nikki pulled out the chair across from Malcolm and sat down. She glanced from left to right as if someone might be listening and dropped the volume of her voice down to a whisper, "It was the article about your last film… and I don't care what the critics said about it, I thought it was fantastic."*

*Malcolm let out a broad smile. It was a compliment his ego so desperately needed to hear after the ridicule and negative feedback he'd been getting from his first studio-directed movie. Hopefully it wouldn't be his last.*

*"Thank you very much. You just might be my only fan out there, I wish everyone thought that, including my agent… or ex-agent," Malcolm said as he admired her flawless skin and beautiful teeth. He couldn't stop staring at her face that had him captivated.*

*"Well, they just don't know talent when they see it."*

*Malcolm smiled again as he nodded his head, was this chick hitting on me? God I hope so, he proclaimed in his head. Malcolm cleared his throat, "So, did you come to LA to be an actor?"*

*"No, I'm a writer, I hope to be the next Shonda Rhimes. My mom hopes I meet some creepy guy that has me running back home."*

*"That is possible out here. Not that I am that creepy guy."*

*"You don't look that creepy," Nikki said as she played with her sandy brown hair that hung just past her shoulders.*

*"Where is home?"*

*"Chicago."*

*"Chicago, wow! City or suburbs?"*

*"Inner city."*

*"You don't strike me as an inner city girl."*

*"I get that a lot, no offense taken." They stared at each other. Malcolm felt himself getting excited and took a deep breath.*

*"So, the next Shonda Rhimes. Well if that happens promise me you will hire me to direct a few episodes."*

*Nikki stood back up and grabbed Malcolm's empty mug, "Please, you will be too big for my show."*

*Malcolm beamed from ear to ear, where did she come from?*

*Nikki gestured to Malcolm's empty mug, "Let me get that refill for you."*

*"Thank you, I appreciate that."*

*Nikki turned and took two steps. Malcolm dropped his left hand sliding his wedding band off and tucking it into his pocket.*

*"Nikki..."*

*She stopped and turned around, "Yes."*

*"Maybe we could go grab lunch when you get off."*

*"I would love that but...I don't have lunch with married men."*

*Malcolm chuckled, "Now who said anyone was married?"*

*"Your article in Write on. I'll bring you that coffee."*

*Nikki turned and walked away as Malcolm laughed to himself.*

Malcolm left the cafe that day but couldn't get Nikki out of his mind. He knew from their ten minute conversation that he had to have her and he knew if he played his cards right that he could eventually break her down... and he did.

"A penny for your thoughts?" Nikki pulled Malcolm back in as she slid back into the bed next to him.

"Huh?"

"Where are you? You thinking about your meeting?"

Malcolm swallowed hard as his memory rewound to his unsuccessful attempt at securing distribution for his new film, "Fuck those white boys. I don't know who the hell to trust anymore, seems as if everyone wants a piece of my dad."

Malcolm took another drag off his cigarette. Nikki grabbed it out of his hand and put the tiny butt out in the ashtray beside the bed.

"He was a legend and you are his son."

Malcolm shook his head as Nikki's lips parted producing a smile across her delicate face, caught in a moment. "Man, my mom was so in love with your dad, she would die if she knew I was sleeping with his son who looked just like him."

"He was a fucking asshole, that's what he was."

"But he was *your* dad. I think you are being too hard on him," Nikki said as she grabbed another cigarette, lighting it up and taking a long drag from it.

Smoke bellowed out from her mouth and nostrils as she licked her dry lips, "I wish I had a father for even a day. My dad jumped ship before I was even born, never knew who he was. All I have is a stupid picture of him. He could be dead now for all I know."

Malcolm laid back onto the pillow, glanced at the clock, knew he should be preparing for Alex's birthday tonight, felt a tightness in his chest just thinking about being festive, social, nice. *Fuck.*

"You're probably better off," Malcolm said as he swung his legs off the low bed and stood with a grunt, walking to gather his clothes. He checked his phone and noticed a missed call from Alex. He quickly cleared his history as he tucked his phone back into his pocket and slid on his pants.

"What are you doing?"

"I gotta go."

Nikki sat up, and dropped her half smoked cigarette in the astray beside her, "You just got here."

"I told you, tonight's my wife's birthday... thing."

"You said that wasn't until eight and it's only three-thirty. Come back to bed. I'm not done with you yet."

Just those words made Malcolm's dick hard, but he knew he had to get Alex a present, he couldn't go home empty handed.

"Rain check."

"Fine, but Malcolm, we need to talk about our future."

Malcolm ignored Nikki as he dressed, then looked back at her laying naked in the bed. The future he thought, something he tried not to predict.

"I'll call you later." Malcolm walked over and kissed her on the forehead.

Malcolm heard a long sigh coming from behind him as he turned to see Nikki in tears.

"Seriously Nik, don't do this, not now."

"I don't complain about you being married, never have, I know my reality is I fell in love with a married man. I just would like a little more time with you, is that so bad to ask?"

Malcolm stopped and thought about how he was playing with fire, again. He thought about how he was juggling two lives, and wondered when they might collide. All he could do was watch his steps and cover his tracks until a better solution presented itself.

Malcolm finished getting dressed and walked back over to where Nikki sat, her knees to her chest and the sheet now covering up her naked body.

"I'm only one person, Nik..." He stroked the side of her face, "...take it or leave it."

Malcolm stood, "I will catch up with you later."

He grabbed his bag, turned and walked out, shutting the door firmly behind him.

Nikki sat in silence feeling as if the room was closing in all around her. She wiped the tears from her face, reached over and lit up another cigarette. *Take it or leave it,* she thought, Malcolm's words echoed in her head before finding their way out of her mouth, "Take it or leave it, huh?" Nikki's eyes narrowed turning from light green to dark, "Well guess what Malcolm Monroe, I'm going to take it… all."

# TEN

Malcolm didn't know what to expect from Alex when he walked into their home. Fortunately, the confrontation was delayed as he was greeted by a bevy of caterers and workers for Alex's 40th birthday.

As the two men, three women team bustled around the first floor house in preparation for the night, Malcolm dropped his soft leather briefcase by the door, kicked off his camel colored Gucci suede shoes and headed up the winding staircase to the second floor.

Malcolm took his strides toward their master bedroom, his feet padding softly on the dark cherry wood floors beneath him. He stopped just short of the white double doors with engraved paneling and reminded himself that this was Alex's night. He swallowed hard, checked his breath making sure there was no remnant of tobacco on it while trying his best to put the thoughts of his shitty meeting behind him as well as their early argument. He turned the silver nob and walked through the door.

A soft lavender scent tickled his nostrils as he felt the heat from an almond scrub shower cascade around him. He took two more steps into the room as Alex's naked body came into view, standing inside the bathroom. She was slowly and methodically applying her body oil to her already glistening chocolate brown skin. It was a daily ritual that she took very seriously, but tonight made her rituals even more important. His eyes flowed over her well-toned body and smiled, remembering the first time he laid eyes on Alex and he knew she would be Mrs. Monroe. He truly loved Alex with all his heart, he just hated how his frustrations with life sometimes got in the way, tainting his true feeling at times as well as altering his actions.

Malcolm took another step as the wood floors shot out a high pitched screech under him, making Alex turn and take notice of his presence. Malcolm swallowed, feeling a wave of uncertainty wash over him.

"Hey," Alex breathed out, grabbing her silk robe and sliding it over her body.

"Hey," Malcolm replied as he stood a few feet from the half opened door. Silence filled the gap between them, each of them at a loss for words. The argument from this morning was still lingering in both their minds, and pulling on their hearts.

"So um… how did your meeting go?" Alex walked out of the bathroom as she tied the belt on her white silk robe in a neat knot across her waist. She headed towards the bed where her outfit was laid out and ready to wear for the night. "I tried to call you earlier to see but you didn't pick up so I--"

"Oh… It was good," Malcolm said cutting her off, then nodded his head, looking away then back towards Alex. He felt a small patch of heat blow across the back of his neck as the restlessness in his stomach reminded him about his uncertain future.

"Good as in… you got distribution?"

Malcolm bit down hard on his lip. He hated to have to tell Alex that he'd dropped the ball yet again and especially hated to have to see that disappointed look on her face, but mostly, he hated the fact that he looked like such a failure in her eyes.

"Yeah, we um…we actually got it," Malcolm said, allowing the lie to fall from his thoughts to his lips, landing on Alex's ears.

Alex threw her arms up with excitement as a smile danced across her face, "Oh my God, Malcolm, that's wow, that's great," Alex squealed as she rushed towards Malcolm wrapping her arms around his stiff body, but then quickly pulling back, "What's wrong, I thought you'd be thrilled? I mean with the distribution deal, that's money coming our way, and a potential deal for another, movie?"

"Let's not get too excited, Alex, one step at a time, okay?"

"I know, but this is what you wanted though, right?"

Malcolm rubbed his head, felt an aching pain in his neck, a dryness on his tongue. "Yeah, of course, no, I'm good," Malcolm forced out a smile as he rubbed the pain that just developed in his neck, "just a lot on my mind with the party and you know, my dad."

Malcolm's eyes floated around the room, hitting the light turquoise walls and matching curtains that were a tone darker before landing back on Alex's face. The lies continued to fall from his mouth, and he hoped

Alex wouldn't see the truth, the pain and the built up frustration from his day.

"Well now we have two things to celebrate tonight."

"Right," Malcolm held onto his forced smile, knowing good and well if he had actually gotten his distribution deal he would be flying on cloud nine, but as it stood, the way he felt, he just wanted to tell the whole world to go to hell.

Malcolm took a few steps over to the six drawer mahogany dresser as he began to take off his watch, jacket and shirt followed by his jeans. Silence took over the room as neither one of them had anything to say. Malcolm felt the knot in his neck begin to pulsate. He took a deep breath, swallowing the tension that was slowly building in him. He looked up to catch Alex staring his way, "Is there anything else wrong?"

"No, babe, I'm fine really. It's just a small headache. Nothing a few aspirin won't cure."

She looked away, then untied her robe, letting it drop to the floor as she reached out to grab her turquoise tank dress with white accents to slide it on. She walked over to her dresser next to Malcolm and begun to dig through her jewelry box. She stopped and turned back to him.

"So are *we* good? I mean this morning was…"

"Yeah, it's cool, Alex. I just um… overreacted." Malcolm raked his fingers through his low twist. "It's your day and I want you to be happy." Malcolm pushed out yet another forced smile as he headed toward their walk-in closet.

Alex smiled and sighed in relief, "Thanks, sweetie."

Alex slid in her gold diamond hoops and threw on her matching gold bangles, turning to face Malcolm again, "So, I wanted to talk to you about something."

Malcolm continued to shift through his various shirts, all organized by color, searching for the right top to compliment the dark jeans he had draped over his arm. Malcolm heard Alex's request but chose to ignore her. The last thing he wanted to do right now was talk.

"Did you hear me?"

Malcolm pulled a light blue shirt off the hanger as he looked over in Alex's direction, eyes connecting once again, "Yeah, can we um, talk later? I really need to grab a shower before the party."

Alex looked away then back at him, uncertainty covered her face, "Sure, of course, it can wait."

"Thanks," Malcolm said. As he headed out the closet, he brushed past Alex and threw his clothes on their ivory leather chaise by the window. He took two more steps towards the bathroom, before turning around and stepping close to her.

"Happy Birthday babe," Malcolm said, and as he looked into Alex's face then pulling her close to him, "I love you."

Alex smiled, gave Malcolm a soft kiss on the lips, "I love you more."

Malcolm continued to stare into Alex's eyes before letting out a soft sigh, "I better get ready," he said, then turned to enter the bathroom before closing the door behind him.

Malcolm felt himself wanting to break down, and wanted to hit something but he kept it together. He felt the anger pacing within him like a bull waiting to be released. He reached for the glass in front of him and pulled underneath, revealing a medicine cabinet, grabbing the Tylenol and just staring at it. Malcolm shook his head and placed the bottle back on the shelf as he slowly closed the mirror door back catching his reflection. He then bent down opening the door to the cabinet below him, reaching way back until he found what he was searching for.

He pulled out a small blue bag and opened it. He reached in the bag and pulled out an electronic cigarette and took two long drags as he closed his eyes savoring the effect and the moment, feeling his body letting go of the stress and frustration that consumed him. He knew he could never smoke a real cigarette in the house since Alex was extremely allergic to the smoke, so he had to find an alternative, one that would keep her suspicion out of the equation. Malcolm took a few more drags before returning the electronic device back into its little blue bag and hiding it back under the bathroom sink.

Twenty minutes later, Alex was putting the finishing touches on her makeup as she sat at her ivory desk with studio lights glaring down on her. Her flawless skin didn't need much but just enough to accentuate her natural beauty, high cheek bones and big almond eyes accented with longer than normal lashes. As she picked up her eyebrow brush to give her brows one last finishing touch, she heard the doorbell ring.

Her eyes diverted over to the clock sitting on her bedside table. 6:45, it had to be her best friend Sylvia, always the first guest to arrive. Sylvia was infamous for being prompt and always had been. Alex's mind drifted back to when she first met Sylvia...

*Alex was surprised when Malcolm told her that her soon-to-be brother-in-law was now dating his publicist. Lance was never the one to mix business with pleasure, but I guess this woman must have been something special. When they arrived at the restaurant, Alex couldn't believe Lance and his date were already there. Lance was notoriously late for everything, although as the night progressed and she got to know Lance's new girlfriend Sylvia, she realized it was her doing all along.*

*Alex's first thought about Sylvia was that she could be great for Lance, she was outspoken, very attractive and smart and could go toe to toe with Lance like a pro. She was a no nonsense type of girl, a refreshing change from the airheads Lance usually brings around. That night Alex and Sylvia talked like old girlfriends and their connection was instant. Alex knew in that moment Sylvia was the kind of friend she wanted to have in her life even if she and Lance didn't make it.*

The doorbell rang for a second time. Alex stood and gave herself one last glance in their full length mirror next to the walk-in closet. Her size eight figure in her turquoise dress brought a satisfying smile to her face. After years of being overweight, coupled with her own self-esteem issues, Alex decided to take matters into her own hands and start her journey to a slimmer body and positive mentality. She was a big advocate of mind over matter and applied it to everything in her life, professionally. Now it was time to make it work for her personal life. She needed this change if not for the mere fact of recognizing herself as the dynamic woman that she was always meant to be, but couldn't seem to push past those extra pounds.

She'd always wanted to run a marathon and that was what had originally set her on a path of fitness. Now three marathons and sixty pounds later, Alex could say she was healthier, happier and a lot more confident after years of feeling lesser than and not equal to women half her stature, all because of her weight. Although Alex had come a long way in the self-esteem department, there were times where she felt her insecurities creep in the back door and most of those had to do with her relationship with Malcolm.

"Hey babe?" Alex shouted through the closed door, "I'm sure that's Sylvia, gonna head down stairs?" Alex stood there waiting for a response but only heard the sound of the racing water from their spa shower.

Alex picked up her phone from her make-up table and shot him a text, only to hear it beep in his pants pocket that laid on the floor where he dropped them. Alex walked over to his pants and pulled out Malcolm's cell; she saw that Malcolm had three unread texts.

She held her breath and glanced back at the bathroom door, where she could hear the water still going. The temptation of snooping tugged on her emotions as the memory of Malcolm's infidelity slid to the forefront of her mind. Alex stared at the blinking icon until the doorbell rang again, snapping her out of her trance. Alex's lips parted as she pushed out the air she was holding, then placed Malcolm's phone on the neatly made bed. She then picked up his pants and shirt that laid on the floor to toss them into the hamper when a small box fell out of his pants pocket and hit the floor. Alex bent down and picked up the box, she opened it to see a pair of diamond earrings glistening back up at her. A smile overtook her face as a sense of relief floated through her body, *I guess Malcolm didn't forget her birthday after all.* She tucked the box back into his pants, giving him the opportunity to give it to her when he was ready. She then laid his pants back where he left them and headed out of the room.

Alex made her way down the hallway, moving to the circular staircase that dropped her into an open foyer with high ceilings and a five tier crystal chandelier smiling down on her. The white marbled floors echoed under her two inch heels as she swung the front door open as her mouth dropped simultaneously. A large gasp followed as Alex laid eyes on an unexpected party guest.

"Reagan?" Alex exclaimed.

"Surprise." Reagan Collins, Alex's younger cousin, stood just outside their door, with a smile on her face and her arm open wide.

"Oh my God!" Alex lunged forward to give Reagan a warm hug. She pulled back, still holding onto her cousin with her hands, "What in the world are you doing in California?"

Reagan beamed from ear to ear as Alex took a step back to let her in. "How could I miss my favorite cousin's 40th birthday party?"

"Oh gawd, I cannot believe I am 40," Alex squealed out.

"Girl please, I could wish to look half as good as you when I hit that age."

"When did you get in?" Alex slowly closed the door behind her, still smiling uncontrollably.

"Last night. Malcolm sent me a message through Facebook a few weeks ago about your dinner party and well, I just had to fly back for it."

Alex playfully planted her right hand on her right hip, "You flew back just for me?" Alex said adding a twisted grin to her suspicion, she knew her cousin better than she knew herself.

Reagan tilted her head to the side, and gave Alex a sheepish smile, "Weeeelll… you and the fact that my assignment had just ended. But everything happens for a reason."

"Uh, huh, that and the declining job market."

They shared a laugh as Reagan followed Alex through the foyer and down a few steps to their state-of-the-art kitchen.

"Omygoodness, did you guys remodel in here? It looks fantastic." Reagan marveled at the chocolate brown cabinets with frosted glasses highlighted by interior lighting. Stainless steel appliances and glistening white marble countertops.

Alex stopped short of their center island. "About a month ago, it was time for a change and well I just did it. My early 40th birthday gift to me."

"But you don't cook."

"Technicalities, my dear, although the person I hired does and now they can do it in style," Alex said with a wink. "I am so glad you are here, how long will you be staying?"

"You know me. A week, a month, a year."

"So no real job prospects yet?"

"I'm working on it," Reagan shot back with an assuring grin.

Alex headed to the fridge and opened it as a gust of cold air hit her bare legs and arms. She grabbed a bottle of wine and laid it on the island counter, then reached over to swipe two glasses hanging like low fruit from their wine stand. Alex raised one glass in the air towards, Reagan, "Wine, hun?"

"Oh no thanks, I gave up drinking eight months ago."

"Really? I wish I had that will power. What brought that on?" Alex said as she twisted the cork screw into the top of the bottle.

"I was just ready to make a change in my life. I also gave up meat. I'm a vegan now."

Alex pulled out the cork, "O-kay? The Reagan I knew couldn't get enough of Porky the pig."

"Yeah, well not anymore."

"Good for you."

"There is one more... thing."

Alex stopped mid pour of her white wine as both her eyebrows shot up, eyes wide as they focused on Reagan's next words.

"Okay?"

"I decided to come out."

"Shut up. That is awesome hun," Alex said as she finished her pour then setting the bottle back down on the white marble counter. "I am so happy for you." Alex always knew Reagan was gay since they were young girls, as beautiful as she was, Reagan never really took full interest in boys like she did.

"Thank you, I know I swore you to secrecy, but now you can tell the world."

"Speaking of the world," Alex's eyes narrow, "Does *she* know?"

Reagan shook her head no, "I haven't spoken to her since I left. Will she be here tonight?"

"Supposed to be, but you know how she is."

"Right." Reagan looked down then back up; Alex could tell there was something there, something left unresolved, but nothing she dared to venture into at the moment.

"Well you look happy that's for sure," Alex said.

"That's because I met someone," Reagan said as a light blush canvased her butterscotch face as she looked down then back up.

"In India?"

"Actually in London, she was there on work and I was finishing up my assignment there. She actually dropped me off."

"Why didn't you bring her in, to meet us?"

"She'll be back a little later, she had some work to finish up, so..." Reagan's voice drifted off, a smile emerging on her face.

"I can't wait to meet her, I'm sure she is amazing if she caught your eye," Alex said, a proud smile flashed over her face.

"Yeah, she's kinda spectacular."

"How did my aunt and uncle receive the news?"

"Surprisingly well. Although my mom is still processing the whole girl-on-girl thing, I don't think she quite understands how the sex thing works."

Alex laughed out loud at the thought of her Aunt Beatrice trying to figure out how two women have sex, though she was sure that her uncle was helping her to understand. Alex briefly thought back to when Reagan found her dad's porn collection under his mattress. Most of it had consisted of women on women, but the total collection could have wall papered their two thousand square foot home.

"I am sure auntie will come around."

"Hey, hey now," Malcolm's voice bolstered behind them as he walked into the kitchen, clearly in a better mood than when Alex left him upstairs. "If it isn't my favorite cousin-in-law,"

"Hey love," Reagan beamed at Malcolm before glancing Alex's way. The message unspoken. *Should she tell him she was out now?* Alex raised an eyebrow but said nothing.

"So what's new with you Miss Photographer? How was India?"

"India was amazing, and... I'm a lesbian now."

Malcolm looked at Alex, then back at Reagan. A bigger smile shot across Malcolm's face, "Nice. Congratulations, although I knew already."

Reagan shot Alex a look.

"What?" Alex said, defenses up.

"Oh, don't think Alex told me, because she didn't. It doesn't take a private eye to see you were playing for the other team. As fine as you are, you should have had brothers working a revolving door, but you didn't, what you did have were the hottest girlfriends. Dead giveaway," Malcolm laughed out loud. "Dead giveaway."

"Malcolm!"

"What babe? I mean come on, like that one friend Charlie, please tell me you got with her? I would have paid to see that."

"Malcolm!"

"What? I'm a guy and two hot girls together is the shit!"

"Thanks Malcolm, that makes me feel even better now."

"It should, matter of fact--"

The doorbell rang, interrupting Malcolm's Penthouse fantasies.

Alex jumped in, "Okay, would you just go get the door? That's probably Sylvia, you know she's always early."

"And miss this tantalizing lesbian conversation?"

Alex shot Malcolm a look.

"Fine, but we are not even close to being done talking about this."

"Go get the door, please."

"Alright, alright." Malcolm headed out the kitchen as he continued to envision Reagan with her friend Charlie as he shook off the image before opening the door. Standing front and center was indeed Sylvia, but what made Malcolm gasp as if someone had just sucker punched him to the gut was what he saw coming up the walkway to his home.

# ELEVEN

*What the fuck was Nikki doing here?* Malcolm heard his inner voice scream out in protest. Malcolm blinked a few times, making sure that what he saw was true and not a figment of his imagination, although after a few seconds, it was clear that his girlfriend was just steps away from his front door and getting closer by the second. Malcolm felt his jaw clamp down as a piercing pain shot through his cheek. *This is not happening, not today.*

A comfortable smile was plastered on Nikki's face as she walked arm and arm with Davis Michael, undoubtedly her date for the evening. Davis was an up and coming actor Malcolm used in his last film. He found Davis through a last minute casting call when his original actor fell through. Davis was not only talented, he had the perfect look for the part, tall, slim and boyishly handsome; he was mistaken for Shemar Moore at times.

As the content couple approached the door, Malcolm and Nikki's eyes met briefly until he found himself yanked out of his momentary horror by the sound of Sylvia's voice.

"Are you gonna just stand there with a stick up your ass or are you going to let us in?" Sylvia asked through her sarcastic grin.

Malcolm's eyes narrowed. There were two things in life Malcolm couldn't stand, stray cats and Sylvia Batista, but unfortunately for him she was Alex's best friend and the one thing he couldn't kill with a BB gun.

"Yeah… yeah, come in," Malcolm grunted as he shifted his body to the side to allow Sylvia to step past him followed by Davis and finally Nikki. The familiar floral scent of Nikki's perfume stroked his senses, as they exchanged a telling glance.

"So where's my BFF?" Sylvia interjected, pulling Malcolm's attention away from Nikki and onto her.

"Kitchen," Malcolm quickly replied to Sylvia, not bothering making eye contact, keeping his undivided attention on the couple in front of him.

Sylvia turned and headed through the foyer towards the kitchen without so much as a thank you.

"So what's going on Mr. Director, what's new?"

"Davis, my man, so glad you could make it."

"Of course, thank you for the invite my brother. Oh, where are my manners?" Davis turned to Nikki. "Malcolm this Nikki Bryant, Nikki, the great Malcolm Monroe. Remember the film I told you I was in?" Davis asked Nikki.

She nodded, the ends of her mouth curled up slightly, "Of course…"

"This is the director," Davis continued, sounding excited.

"It is very nice to meet you, Malcolm." Nikki tilted her head slightly to the left, holding her smile front and center. Malcolm scanned Nikki's deliciously perfect body, all tucked into her perfect short black dress, in what was now turning into the most less-than-perfect night.

"Same here," Malcolm stammered. His eyes were locked in a tug of war with hers, trying to decipher her thought and motives.

Davis clapped his hands together, shaking them out of their trance, "The birthday girl is in the kitchen?"

Malcolm's eyes darted over to Davis, "She is, go on in there, I will join you guys in a minute."

"Sounds good my brother," Davis gave Malcolm a friendly pound on the side of his shoulder, as he scanned him from head to toe, "We gotta rap later, but looking good brother."

"Yeah… thanks."

Davis then placed his hand on the small of Nikki's back as he lead her out of the foyer, with Malcolm's eyes absorbing their move, step and interaction.

As they got a few feet away, Nikki glanced back over her shoulder to Malcolm as he mouthed to her, "What are you doing here?"

"I was invited by my date," Nikki gave Malcolm a half smile and a wink before turning her head around as she walked side by side with Davis towards the kitchen.

Malcolm stood in the same spot in which he originated upon opening the door. He heard the chatter of the new guests' arrival in the kitchen as he then began to pace in a small radius in the foyer, heart racing, temper rising. *Shit.*

He raked his fingers through his small twist, as his hand fell to the back of his neck, D*ammit*. Then he dropped his hand down to his side with a loud slap on his pants. *What the fuck.*

Malcolm couldn't pinpoint his rage. He couldn't decide whether it was the fact that Nikki was at his wife's birthday party or that she was here with another man. *Did she come on purpose to try and force his hand into making a decision? Was this some kind of set up? Was Davis in on this as well?* Malcolm couldn't stop the questions from flooding his thoughts, he needed to figure out what was happening and shut this down now.

Malcolm took a few deep breaths forcing himself to breathe easily through his mouth, then methodically walked back into the kitchen to see everyone in casual conversation. He lingered by the door as he observed the actions of Alex, while keeping an extra eye on Nikki and Davis.

Malcolm swallowed slowly, a dry lump rose and fell in his throat. He needed a drink. He walked to the fridge and pulled out a beer, determined to keep his eyes pinned on the social interaction going on before him. The hustle and bustle of the small but capable wait staff moving unobtrusively in and out the kitchen preparing for the upcoming dinner didn't shake his focus, not one bit. He kept a steady eye and an open ear.

Malcolm leaned against the counter just next to the fridge as he reached in the drawer next to him, grabbing a beer opener and popping off the top. He took a long swig, feeling his body temperature dropping down a few degrees as the bitter sweet taste of his liquid libation sailed through his mouth, tantalizing his taste buds before flowing down his throat.

"So Nikki, are you from LA?" Malcolm felt a surge of discomfort when he heard Alex directing a question to Nikki.

Nikki shifted in her place before throwing on a pleasant smile, "No, I'm actually from Chicago."

"I love Chicago," Reagan chimed in, "What brought you to LA?"

"I'm, um, I'm actually an aspiring television writer."

"Very cool. Any luck so far?" Reagan continued as she nibbled on a few carrot sticks from the veggie tray on the center island.

"No, not yet. It's only been a year since I moved out here, but I'm making some interesting contacts," Nikki said, shooting Malcolm a quick glance before bringing her attention back to Reagan.

"She's not half bad either," Davis said, directing his eyes to Nikki, "You know I would tell you the truth, right?"

Nikki just smiled, "Of course, baby."

Malcolm felt his gut drop and his jaw clenched hearing the small term of endearment between the two.

"So how did you guys meet?" Alex asked.

Davis looked at Nikki as a small smile emerged from his face.

"A cafe right here in Sherman Oaks, actually."

"Oh, which one?"

"Michelle's cafe on Moorpark, I actually work there," Nikki interjected.

Alex stopped what she was doing, as her brows came together as if one, "Isn't that where you write, babe?" Alex said directing her question to Malcolm.

*Shit.* Malcolm felt another pull in his stomach, this time a stronger more powerful one, he shifted, body weight as he pushed himself to stand straight up, taking another slow sip of his beer, feeling a rage building in him.

"Malcolm?"

"Yeah, what's up?" Malcolm looked up, as if he wasn't tuned into the conversation around him, and saw all eyes on him, including Nikki's.

"Where are you?"

Malcolm shrugged his shoulders, "I'm right here." Malcolm gave Alex a slightly annoyed response with an even more annoyed look. "What's up?"

"Isn't that where you write?"

"Where's that?" Malcolm threw out a question to Alex's question, his quick attempt to vibe for more time.

"Michelle's cafe?"

"Yeah, yeah, why?" Malcolm rattled back.

"Nikki just said she works there. Have you guys met before?"

Malcolm shifted in place, felt a small cluster of sweat surface on his back, and time seemed to stand still as everyone awaited his answer, even Nikki.

"Actually, no not to my knowledge. You know me babe, when I'm there I have on blinders. I'm in my zone," Malcolm gave a half smile before throwing the rest of his beer down his throat. Without a response, Alex focused her attention back to Reagan and Sylvia. Nikki and Malcolm made eye contact, as Malcolm's eyes narrowed, he slowly shook his head back and forth. Nikki looked away amused.

"Yo, can I get one of those brew-skies you're sipping on?" Davis said, walking over to Malcolm.

"Yeah, of course, actually I have some more at the bar on the patio."

"Babe," Alex looked up, "Davis and I are gonna head out to the patio, little bit too much estrogen in here for me? You need anything?"

"No, I'm good, thanks hun," Alex responded.

Malcolm turned to leave only to be stopped dead in his tracks by Sylvia's knowing glare. One thing Malcolm knew about his relationship with his wife's best friend is that she rarely missed a beat.

They continued to hold a stare before Malcolm broke the invisible hold turning to head out the kitchen, Davis in tow. He glanced back to see Sylvia's eyes filled with a growing satisfaction and a knowing smile.

Malcolm stepped behind the outside bar and grabbed two beers, cracked them open handing one to Davis before he took a seat on their outside living room. It was comfortably equipped with two chairs and a couch centered around a large fire pit. Malcolm snagged the cushioned chair facing the door while Davis sat on the adjoining couch.

"Now this is what I call a fly ass outside set up," Davis said, taking a sip of his beer. He looked around, admiring Malcolm's custom designed backyard with in-ground swimming pool, waterfall and inside/outside kitchen. It was all accented by the large French doors that lay open to the side allowing for an easy inside outside flow, perfect for any type of party.

"Thanks, but it's a work in progress."

"Looks like a finished progress to me." Davis continued to admire Malcolm's backyard before turning his attention back to him, "So what's up with the film? You mentioned you were going after distribution?"

Malcolm felt a twitch in his back. He should have known the subject would come up during the night, especially since Davis was one of his actors in the film.

"It's cool man. We are close to getting a deal."

"Really? Like how close?" Davis sat up a bit on his seat.

"Like in the next few weeks close, I'd say."

Davis did a small fist air pump. "Hell yeah, that's music to my ears."

"Yeah, it's a process, that..." Malcolm's voice trailed off as he noticed Nikki walking out of the kitchen and into the living room, followed by Sylvia. Davis turned to see what just caught Malcolm's attention, then back at Malcolm.

"So what do you think of my date?" A smile danced across Davis' face as he stared at Nikki from afar, licking his lips in anticipation of what the night could bring with her.

Malcolm felt a surge of jealously run through his body. "Yeah, she's um, she's cool." Malcolm took a sip of his beer, "You been dating long?" Malcolm inquired as he propped one foot up on the ledge of his fire pit.

"Not long, but let's just say she is a top candidate."

"Wow, okay…" Malcolm adjusted himself in his chair, "I thought you had a girl."

"I do, but come on yo, you know how it is in LA, the more the merrier, right?"

Malcolm took a swig of his beer as he sneaked a quick glance of Nikki chatting with Sylvia on the couch, "Hey, I'm not mad at that."

"So what's up? Working on anything new?" Malcolm inquired, trying to find focus in his conversation but it was hard, damn hard.

Davis leaned back again in his chair. "Life is good man, can't complain. Booked a McDonald's spot just yesterday."

"Congrats yo, that's what I'm talking about." Malcolm said only giving Davis half his attention as he threw glances back into the house, keeping an eye on the female interaction between Sylvia and Nikki.

"Couldn't have come at a better time. A brother was hurting."

Malcolm nodded his head, "Yeah man, it's rough out here…"

"Yeah, like you would know," Davis said as he gave Malcolm's house another once over with his eyes. "How many bedrooms do you have here?" Davis threw out.

Malcolm looked away then back at Davis, "Five."

"Nice. So you're sitting on about 10,000 sq. feet of home?"

Malcolm felt himself getting irritated by Davis' curiosity of his home.

"Yeah, roughly."

"Cool, cool." A silence dropped between them, "So how long have you and Alex lived here? I love Sherman Oaks, by the way, I hear the schools are great out here."

"I grew up in this house."

Davis sat up on the edge of the couch, "Hold up, so this is your dad's house, the legendary Langston Monroe?"

"No, it's my house."

"But it was his house, right?"

Malcolm threw on a calming smile, *this is why I don't invite broke ass actors into my space,* Malcolm thought. But inviting Davis had been Alex's choice. She'd taken a liking to Davis and thought it would be nice to include him, "It's my fucking house, okay?"

Malcolm locked eyes with Davis as he slowly sat back on the couch, "Right, of course." Davis looked away, slowly sipping his beer and stood, "Yo, I'm gonna go check on my date, but it was cool rapping with you."

"Yep," Malcolm said, crossing his right leg over his left.

"Catch up with you later," Davis goes to pat Malcolm on the shoulder but stopped short, pulling his hand down to his side. He turned and headed through the open white French doors and into the living room where he took a seat next to Nikki.

Malcolm swallowed hard as he stood, shook off his frustration with the conversation, with his life. He walked over to the edge of their heated pool with attached hot tub. The sun was slowly descending on the other side of the trees as a soft breeze tickled his ears. The night was only beginning, but he felt like it would be a millennium before it all came to an end; he just hoped he could keep it together until then.

# TWELVE

Sylvia prided herself on never missing a beat, but when it came to Malcolm's devious way, she had learned to turn the other cheek, for reasons she could never utter, for reasons beyond her control. From the moment Nikki walked into the house with Davis, Malcolm had never been more jittery. Trepidation dripped off of him like sweat beads in a sauna. To her, that was a telltale sign that something was up.

Sylvia took one last sip of her Perrier sparkling water before placing the bottle down on the white square leather coaster that sat on the edge of the glass cocktail table. She sat back and continued to observe Malcolm and Nikki. The discomfort, the quick unassuming glances that bounced back and forth between them; it was clear that something was going on between the two. It was nearly enough to give whoever witnessed their interactions whiplash.

Sylvia watched Malcolm's every move from where she sat, just a few feet away on the caramel-colored sectional in the spacious living room with a wood burning fireplace. The periodic glances into the house, the shifting of his feet and excess drinking. Sylvia shook her head, gave it more thought, felt the nausea return to her stomach again.

The soft tones of Ne-yo floated in the air as Sylvia's mind continued to churn, producing her own scenarios and conclusions. She finally stood, smoothed out her black pencil line skirt and ruffled buttoned-up top and took her strides in her three inch heels across the dark black wood living room floor. She gently stepped out onto the patio as the fresh air greeted her with a smile.

Sylvia positioned herself next to Malcolm, as she just stood next to him not saying one word. It was evident that they were not that fond of each other and were always working overtime to keep the peace especially in the presence of Alex.

Malcolm was aware of her presence but decided to ignore it, continuing to look straight ahead. Finally, after the silence became too much, he spoke up, "Can I help you with something?"

"Why do you keep doing this?" Sylvia spoke in a hushed tone.

Malcolm took a deep breath as his eyes closed then opened, "Doing what, Sylvia?" Malcolm replied in his *I could care less*, tone.

"You know what I'm talking about," Sylvia checked her surroundings before speaking her next thought, "You're fucking Davis' date aren't you?"

Malcolm let out a small chuckle, "Wow, can't slip anything by you can I?" He turned towards her, looked at the side of her face, "You would be correct."

Malcolm's eyes became dark, narrowing to half their size, "Although I know my secret is safe with you. Isn't that right?"

Sylvia closed her eyes tight, taking a deep breath, felt the pain mixed with rage and topped off with regret flood her body, "I don't want to play this game anymore. I can't."

Malcolm tilted his head and smiled, "I don't know what you're talking about, Sylvia?"

"You know… exactly what I'm talking about," her voice rose then fell, as she realized she needed to keep what they were discussing between them.

"And what do you propose as a solution?" Malcolm turned his body towards Sylvia as his eyebrow lifted, emphasizing his next statement, "Telling Alex? Because we *both* know that would not end well… for you."

Sylvia bit her bottom lip, thought long and hard at what Malcolm just said; the scenario had crossed her mind a million times before but she knew the ramifications. Whatever way her secret was revealed to Alex, it would end badly, she was sure of that.

"Am I right?" Malcolm asked.

Sylvia swallowed, forced back her tears; years of guilt swelled up inside her like tiny balloons inflating all at once.

"Right," Sylvia managed to whisper.

Malcolm took another swig of his beer, "I thought so. Because if Alex gets wind of *this* or *any* other encounters, I'll be forced to tell her what a wonderful friend you are."

A sharp breath shot out from Sylvia's mouth. At this moment she wanted a drink very badly. It didn't matter that she was pregnant. What mattered was the realization that drinking was what got her into the situation in the first place. Something she vowed to never let happen to her again. Drinking was no longer an option for her, ever.

"It's not right what you are doing," Sylvia finally managed to say.

"Really, and when the fuck did you grow a conscience? Because the last time I checked, you're no better than me."

Sylvia heard a foreign sound escape through her lips, "Please I will never be like you."

"That's right I forgot, you're perfect. So perfect in fact, that you slept with your best friend's husband weeks before his wedding."

Sylvia felt her mouth involuntarily clamp down, her throat dry to the attempt of closure. "That wasn't supposed to happen." Tears raced down her face, dropping to the ground.

"Well, it did, and if you don't want Alex to ever find out, I suggest you continue to keep your big mouth shut. Because we can walk back into that kitchen and lay it all on the table for Alex, every single fine detail."

"We agreed we would never say anything to Alex about that, ever."

"Yes, that we did, but it seems as if you are getting all 'I'm every woman' on my ass so I have to keep that spade in my pocket." Malcolm tapped his right hand on his right jeans pocket, looking at Sylvia, "So tell me, will I have to use it?"

"You have just as much to lose as I do," Sylva shot back, trying to lessen her guilt. She was attempting to gain some courage, but this was her kryptonite. She couldn't battle this. She had no idea how.

“I think she would be a little more forgiving o

backstabbing best friend who should’ve been watch

of sticking a knife in it.”

“I didn’t even know Alex then.”

“But you did know I had a wife. And that certainly didn’t p you from sleeping with your boyfriend’s brother to get back at him.”

“I came to you as a friend to talk about my issues with Lance, to try and get some insight from the one person I thought knew him well.”

“Yeah, right,” Malcolm shook his finger at Sylvia, “I know how you women work, you wanted me from the first time you saw me. And they say men are the fucked up species. Please, you women are sneaky as shit.”

Sylvia felt her knees weaken; she shifted trying to keep herself from breaking, fought to push the rage that was mounting inside. A moment of drunken weakness that ended up in a lifetime of guilt. A moment of vulnerability that lead to the betrayal of her soon-to-be best friend. A moment she so desperately wished she could take back, put down that drink, talk to someone else.

“Ironic how close you two have become, it’s almost laughable. I guess the saying, ‘Be careful who you fuck’ is universal.”

“That wasn’t my intention that night.”

“Well actions definitely spoke louder than words in your case.” Malcolm shook his head and laughed as if he was reminiscing on their events.

“You could have pushed me away.”

"A scorned inebriated woman with no inhibitions?" Malcolm shook his head, "There's no sense in that."

"I was your brother's girlfriend."

"Who was offering up the pussy."

"I was drunk."

"Don't forget desperate."

"I fucking hate you."

"Hey, get in line."

Sylvia stopped, this was going nowhere and she was starting to feel nauseous. Her head began to pound as she broke out in a cold sweat, "Screw you Malcolm."

"No thanks. I don't do seconds."

Sylvia wiped the sweat from her forehead, then turned to leave but stopped, looked at Malcolm, "You just remember, every dog has their day."

"Oh yea, and every bitch has a pussy waiting to be violated."

Sylvia shook her head, "Jackass," before she turned to walk through the glass doors as she attempted to hold back her tears. She looked up to see Alex standing in front of her with a concerned look on her face.

"Sylvia what's wrong?"

Sylvia looked away, saying nothing as she headed off the patio and to the bathroom. Sylvia never wished death on anyone but in that moment she wished he would die.

"Stupid-ass women," Malcolm muttered to himself.

He finished off his beer and tossed it into the small trash can next to the table before turning to see Alex standing behind him.

"Hey, how long have you been standing there?"

"Not long."

Alex walked closer to Malcolm, "What did you say to Sylvia? She looked upset."

Malcolm shrugged his shoulders, "I guess she didn't agree with what I had to say."

"About what?"

"Her divorce with Lance."

"Hun, why are you talking about that with her? We all know you weren't for that marriage in the first place."

"Yeah, for good reason, she's a hoe."

"Okay, you need to stop calling her that."

"Whatever, I don't want to talk about it anyway. So, are you having a good time?"

"I am," Alex said. She wasn't done with him yet, but she'd leave it for now.

Malcolm looked deep into Alex's eyes trying to see if she had any idea of his true relationship with Nikki. "Cool."

Malcolm reached out and pulled Alex into him as he peered over her shoulder to look to see where Nikki was standing.

Alex fell into Malcolm's arms as she wrapped her arms around him, "As far as Sylvia, I do wish you guys would start getting along again. You used to speak so highly of her when she first started dating Lance. You couldn't wait for us to meet."

"Yeah, well that was a long time ago, babe, things change, people change."

Alex smiled up at Malcolm, "Thanks again for doing this party."

"No problem, but I wish you hadn't invited Davis."

Alex turned to look over to where Davis and Nikki sat, "Why? I like him I thought you did too?"

"He's a little annoying, then again most actors are."

"Well his date is gorgeous, huh?"

Malcolm smiled and turned his head slightly to the right, seeing Nikki's glare directed their way.

Malcolm shrugged his shoulders, felt a jealous singe shoot through his body, "Yeah, she's okay."

Alex's eyebrows shot up, "Are you kidding me? She's like 'cover girl' hot. Not to mention her body and that head of hair she has."

"Really Alex? I thought Reagan was the lesbian here?"

Alex pulled back from Malcolm, "I'm just playing around, besides, I wouldn't do anything without you. Although, if I did, would you be mad if I didn't ask you to join us?"

Malcolm jerked away from Alex, "What the fuck is wrong with you?"

"Jesus, Malcolm, what has gotten into you, that was a joke. I thought we were good?"

Malcolm rubbed the back of his neck, "Yeah, we're great, fucking fantastic, Alex.

Malcolm broke away, heading into the house and through the kitchen; he passed Nikki as they exchanged another glance before he headed to his office and shut the door.

Alex watched as Malcolm stormed through the house disappearing around the corner; she couldn't put her finger on what was going on in that head of his, and why he wasn't in a better mood, especially since his distribution deal got green lighted. She also wondered why he had not given her, her gift yet? Was it really for her? That thought triggered her intuition as her mind began to churn. She took a deep breath before taking her casual strides through the house, up the stairs, down the hallway and into their master bedroom. There she noticed Malcolm's pants were gone off the floor. She walked over to Malcolm's hamper, lifting the lid and spotting his faded jeans from earlier in the day. As she pulled them out she noticed the box was gone from his pocket.

"Interesting," she mumbled to herself. "Okay, Alex, the night is not over, don't jump to any conclusions yet," she said as she dropped the pants back into the hamper, closing the top over them. Alex turned to get a glance of herself in their full length mirror as she reminded herself how nothing in life is easy and the great things take work, a lot of work, but she couldn't stop the negative thoughts from attempting to edge out the positive one.

Alex gave herself one last smile as she headed out the bedroom and back down to the party. This night was turning out to be something Alex wished would be over very soon.

# THIRTEEN

"I think you need to put your jacket on," Randolph glanced down at Lacey's low-cut BCBG dress that revealed her perfectly pushed up breasts and defined cleavage. Lacey adjusted herself in the butterscotch leather seats of their Cadillac SUV before glancing down at her 2-carat ring and reminded herself not to throw in the towel just yet.

"I will, I just don't want it to wrinkle in the car," Lacey shot back before turning her head to look out the window.

Satisfied with that answer, Randolph turned his attention back to the road as their truck sailed off the Balboa exit from the 101 freeway. They veered left crossing Ventura Blvd, heading up the winding canyon hills to Malcolm and Alex's home. They continued to ride in silence until, "Lacey, I'm sorry about this morning, I didn't mean for that to happen."

Lacey turned to Randolph, "Yeah, but it did."

"Yes, I understand that... but are you at least willing to take partial responsibility in the outcome?"

Lacey's head snapped back, "Excuse me?"

"Lacey, we had an agreement and you crossed the line."

"Well I am sorry if I wanted to make love to my fiancé, I guess that just makes me human."

"Human we are, which is why we are constantly tested by the devil."

"Okay I don't need a bible verse right now to justify that I was fucking horny. Can we just drop it please," Lacey said as she felt her anger rising from her libido.

Randolph nodded his head, "Okay."

A few minutes later they were cruising down a tree-lined street, passing several exquisite homes all of different sizes and styles before turning into Malcolm and Alex's circular driveway.

Lacey unbuckled her seat belt then looked over at Randolph who had not made a move, "You coming?"

"Yes, I have to call the church. Go on in, I will only be a few minutes."

Lacey opened the door and carefully stepped out of the truck. She placed her Jimmy Choo black pumps on the step riser before hitting the asphalt below. She turned to grab her purse when Randolph pulled his phone away from his ear, "Don't forget your jacket."

*Oh for the love of gawd*, Lacey cussed to herself, "Right, of course," Lacey said, smiling pleasantly as she threw the jacket on, "How's that?"

Randolph winked, "Divine."

Lacey didn't respond. As she closed the door, she caught a glimpse of her coco-colored reflection in the black tinted windows. She admired her newly highlighted hair with added pieces that gave her the volume and length that could give any weave lover an orgasm, not to mention her stylish short bangs that framed the front of her face, accenting her perfectly arched eyebrows and round cheek bones. Lacey had been going to the same Stylist, Kim Kimble, for the last five years and one thing she loved about Miss Kimble was she could do a breathtaking weave. Lacey gave herself one last gander before she turned to head for the front door, retrieving her key, letting herself in the Monroe mansion.

Lacey immediately pulled off her jacket, throwing it on the chaise lounge by the door revealing the form-fitted cocktail dress she'd picked out to show off her perfect figure. Lacey checked out herself once more in the large hallway mirror and pushed her breasts up a notch before heading into the living room.

Several more people had arrived as Lacey made her way to the kitchen when she spotted Alex.

"Happy birthday to yoou, happy birthday to yooou, happy birthday my dear Alex, happy birthday to yooooou..." Lacey sang in a pitch perfect tone. She loved showing off her vocal skills whenever she could, and of course, the attention didn't hurt either.

"Hey hon," Alex said smiling as they embraced. "I'm so glad you could make it. Malcolm said you were going on tour soon."

"Yes, but that isn't until the end of the month."

Alex glanced behind Lacey, "Where is Randolph?"

Lacey waved her left hand in the air, as if dismissing her next statement, "He's in the car on the phone, he'll be in soon, I guess."

Lacey noticed Alex's mouth drop wide open, "Well, I guess I don't have to ask you how it's going," Alex said as she grabbed Lacey's left hand in mid wave as she analyzed the ring on her finger, "You are kidding me!" Lacey noticed Sylvia turn and head over to see what the commotion was.

"You're engaged?" Alex said as her eyes enlarged, waiting for a confirmation.

"I know it's quick but when you know," Lacey's shoulders rose then fell, "you know."

"I guess so, wow," Alex said. She turned to see Sylvia holding Lacey's hand in hers, "Did you see this?"

"Couldn't miss it from across the room. Congratulations, Marcus has great taste."

"Randolph," Lacey said, quickly correcting Sylvia.

"What?" Sylvia threw back.

"Marcus was the *last* guy," Alex jumped in.

"Oh, so when did you start dating…" Sylvia had already forgotten his name.

"Randolph," Lacey said, filling in the blank.

"Right. Clearly I need to come around more often," Sylvia added trying to clean up her slip.

"We've been dating a little over five months, now," Lacey confirmed.

"Okay…" Sylvia shot Alex a sidelong glance then quickly focused her attention back on Lacey. "Hey, if it's meant to be, it's meant to be, right?"

"That's my motto," Lacey said with a smile.

"And what would that be?" A voice from behind interjected.

They turned to see Malcolm standing there. They averted their eyes and no one said anything.

"Oh sure, now the cackling crew wants to clam up," Malcolm said.

"Hey big bro," Lacey smiled.

"What's up sis?" Malcolm said giving Lacey a hug, "Where is Rev Al Sharpton of Woodland Hills?"

"Cute," Lacey said, giving Malcolm a small smile.

"You mean her new fiancé?" Alex said with a broad smile across her face.

"Thanks, Alex," she turned back to Malcolm. "He's parking the car."

A critical grin played its way across Malcolm's face. "Really? Fiancé? Wait, are you trying to break Lance and Sylvia's record?" Malcolm asked.

Sylvia's face screwed up in discontent. "For your information, Malcolm, Lance and I got engaged after dating for *five years*."

"Oh that's right, it was the marriage that only lasted for three months."

Sylvia and Malcolm locked eyes, neither one looking away, "Quite a memory you have there Malcolm. I thought you only focused on yourself."

"Aw snap," Lacey said, enjoying the camaraderie between them, she always had.

"Okay, you two, that's enough," Alex said hoping to create peace. "Lacey, when is the wedding?"

"Oh that's not planned yet, probably sometime after I get back from the tour."

"I've always wanted to date a pastor," Sylvia welcomed a devious smile on her face, "How's the sex?"

"Well it's um," Lacey took a deep breath, *how could she put this?* Everyone stared waiting for an answer.

"Okay we haven't slept together yet."

"Really?" Sylvia said.

"Yeah, we're practicing being celibate until marriage."

Malcolm who was near the fridge, sipping on a newly opened bottle of beer, almost choked upon hearing the word 'celibate' coming out of Lacey's mouth.

"That's a joke right?" Malcolm said, a huge smile blossoming.

"No, Malcolm it is not," Lacey shot back.

"I mean, come on Lace, you being celibate is like asking the pope not to pray."

"It's possible," Lacey threw out a non-convincing rebuttal.

"Not with the Lacey I grew up with. Did I ever tell you the time when we all went away on a camping trip in—"

"Really Malcolm?" Lacey cut him off before he spilled all her business.

Malcolm laughed out loud, "Okay, okay, I believe in you, I do. I also believe the Cleveland Browns can win a Super Bowl in this lifetime!"

"Malcolm stop being so judgmental, people can change, especially if it's for the right person," Alex chimed in.

"I agree with that, although there are those few things that never change," Sylvia declared, directing her intention to Malcolm.

Malcolm just grinned, drinking his beer.

Lacey looked up to see Reagan coming through the door from the hallway, their eyes connected and Lacey felt herself at a loss for words.

"Hey Lacey," Reagan said in a soft tone.

Lacey, who thought Reagan was out of the country, found herself at a loss for words, suddenly seeing her standing in Malcolm and Alex's kitchen, "Well this is a surprise," Lacey finally got out.

"Yeah, I wanted to surprise... Alex for her 40th, and well, here I am."

"How long are you staying?"

Reagan curled her index finger around a lock of curls that hung down to her shoulders, "I will be here for a while," she dropped her hand, then folded her arms in front of her chest, "but who knows with me?"

"Right, of course, well Europe looks good on you, you look..." Lacey scanned her body, *amazing*. "Relaxed."

"Thanks. You look great, did you change your hair?"

"Bangs,"

"Ah," Reagan said as her eyes dropped down to Lacey's ring finger then back up. "So how is your album doing? I actually heard one of your songs playing in London."

"Yeah?"

"Yeah, I think it was *A Different Kind Of Love*."

"Well that's um, that's a good thing. I'm actually getting ready to go on tour in a few months."

"Wow, that's huge," Reagan's voice trailed off as her eyes fell back down to Lacey's ring finger. "So you're—"

Lacey's eyes followed Reagan's, "Engaged, yes," Lacey said, and felt a flush come over her coco skin.

Reagan nodded and forced a smile, "Congratulations."

Lacey grabbed her left finger with her right hand as she began to nervously twist the ring around her finger, "Yeah, thanks."

She dropped her hands back down to her side, "It was pretty sudden, but we knew right away, you know?"

Reagan's head began to nod up and down again, "Right."

Lacey noticed Reagan's eyes float past her as she turned to see Randolph entering the kitchen, "Ah, speak of the devil, here is my fiancé now."

"Hey sorry, my call took longer than I thought," Randolph said as he planted a small kiss on Lacey's cheek, then focused on Reagan.

"Baby, this is Reagan, Alex's… cousin."

"Very nice to meet you, Reagan."

"Likewise, and congratulations by the way," Reagan managed. "Lacey just told me the great news."

"Thank you very much, God is good, we are both very excited, aren't we sweetheart?"

"Oh, over the hill," Lacey said with the tilt of her head.

Reagan smiled as she looked at Lacey. "Well I'm gonna go mingle."

"Of course and I need a drink," Lacey returned pleasantly.

"Not too many now?" Randolph interjected. Lacey decided to ignore his comment, at least in that moment.

"Great seeing you again, Lacey," Reagan said before turning her attention to Randolph, "and very nice meeting you, Randolph."

"Likewise."

Reagan stepped away. Lacey watched her walk and turned to Randolph as his cell phone rang. He felt inside his jacket pocket and glanced at the display.

"Ah, sweetheart, I gotta take this, promise, only a minute," he threw a consolation peck on her cheek and walked into the living room.

Alex stood across the kitchen observing the whole interaction with Lacey, Reagan and Randolph, something that piqued her interest since she knew a little of the background story. Alex grabbed a fresh glass and filled it up with the newly opened bottle of pinot that was sitting on the island, then headed over to where Lacey stood, alone.

"Here ya go," Alex said handing Lacey the wine glass.

Lacey smiled, "Thanks, you must have been reading my mind."

"Well it wasn't your mind that was speaking, you looked very uncomfortable over here."

"No, I'm good," Lacey said as she took a long sip of her wine.

With no one in ear shot, Alex could finally say what she wanted to say from the moment Lacey walked in the house. "Lace, what's going on?"

"What do you mean?"

"We haven't seen you in over four months and then you show up, engaged?"

"So?"

"Well don't you think it's kinda fast, considering..." Alex stopped herself, a small slip of the tongue propelled Lacey to inquire where she was going with this.

"Considering what, Alex?"

Alex took a deep breath, knowing Reagan is gonna kill her, "Lacey, I know, I know about you and Reagan, she told me."

Lacey took another long sip from her glass, "Listen Alex, I don't know what story Reagan has told you, but whatever it is I am sure it's a lie."

Alex nodded her head, she knew denial a mile away. "Right, of course," Alex conceded, she should have known Lacey would not be as open as Reagan. Alex then noticed Lacey glancing over at Reagan lost in her own thoughts.

"You gonna be okay?" Alex asked.

Lacey snapped her head back Alex's way, "Why wouldn't I?" Lacey responded with a more than nice tone.

"You know me, Dr. Monroe, always making sure everyone is A-okay," Alex said trying to lighten a tense moment, although Lacey seemed less than interested in having this conversation with Alex.

Alex's eyes followed Lacey's stare over to Randolph where he paced in a small line, still talking on the phone, "So he's really the one?"

"Definitely," Lacey answered still staring his way.

"You sure? I mean, you said you've only known him for four months, maybe you should take a little more time… see if this is really what you want," Alex said, her eyebrows arching.

Lacey made an annoyed face. "I know what I want Alex, okay?"

Alex gave Lacey a half smile and a slow nod, "Okay, I'm just looking out for you, because I care."

"And I appreciate your concern, but really, I'm good." Lacey turned and looked Alex directly in her eyes, "Can you just be happy for me?"

Alex threw her hand up, "Of course, all I want is for you to be happy," Alex said as she lost Lacey once again, as her attention was snapped up by Reagan socializing from guest to guest.

"I'm gonna go be social with my guests," Alex said, realizing this conversation was going nowhere fast.

"Okay," Lacey smiled Alex's way.

Lacey watched as Alex headed to the living room to greet a few newly arrived guests. Lacey loved Alex, but she got a bit annoying always trying to fix everyone's life. She quickly downed the rest of her pinot, as she walked over to the island to refill her empty glass with more wine. She wondered just how much Reagan told Alex about them, and why she felt the need to even discuss it with her.

The last thing she needed was Alex telling anyone in her family about her relationship with a woman, it wasn't like she was actually gay.

Lacey took another long sip of her wine as she glanced over at Randolph who was still on the phone before turning all her attention to Reagan, her ex-girlfriend.

# FOURTEEN

"What the hell are you doing here?" Malcolm asked in fiery and low tone. He'd finally found an opportunity to talk to Nikki while Alex occupied herself with her many guests.

"Apparently I am wishing your wife a happy 40th," Nikki grinned as she delicately bit into a small egg roll, then placed the rest back down on her small white plate with gold trim. "Mmmm, these are delicious, you wanna bite?"

"This is not a joke, Nikki," Malcolm said, his voice tight with emphasis. As Malcolm continued to talk, he deliberately looked straight ahead so as not to draw too much attention to them, pausing to keep an eye out for Alex as well as any other suspecting eyes.

"Who said it was?" Nikki threw back at Malcolm.

"Then why are you here? Why are you coming in my house, blowing up my spot?" Malcolm added to his flurry of inquiries.

"Really? Is that what you think I am doing? Is that who you think I am?" Nikki scoffed, rolling her eyes and shaking her head.

"The proof is in the motherfucking pudding."

"Seriously Malcolm. If I wanted to blow up your spot I could have done it a long time ago. I don't deserve this from you, I put up with your shit and this is how you treat me?"

"Like my side piece, yes."

Malcolm heard a deliberate hiss escape from Nikki's lips, "Wow, so all that talk was just hot air."

"You knew I was married, so how could that be?" Malcolm uttered.

"I don't know, maybe the dozen times you told me how unhappy you were, how I made you feel like a man when your wife didn't, I guess that was all orgasm talk, huh? God, you are such an asshole, I question, why do I even stay with you?"

Malcolm turned slightly to see Nikki's eyes filling with tears, "Listen, this isn't the place to talk about this. We can talk later," Malcolm said, resuming his forward stance position.

Nikki wiped the tears before they had a chance to run down her cheek, "I'll be busy later," Nikki threw out in a firm tone.

Malcolm felt his jaw tightening hearing her last sentence. Unfortunately, it was also accompanied with a gnawing in his stomach, "Busy…now that is funny." He chuckled then glanced over towards Davis in a casual conversation of his own, focusing everything he had on him.

"I don't know what you see in that cornball."

Nikki laughed, gathered her composure looking down at her black strappy sandals then up into the air before turning her head in Malcolm's direction, "You have no right to be jealous. You're the one that's married, not me."

Malcolm shifted his body from right to left, tucked his hands in the pockets of his black jeans as he threw a full smile on his face, "I think you need to leave."

Nikki turned to look at Malcolm, "And miss all the excitement?" She tilted her head as a dubious smile tap-danced across her face, "Not in a million years."

Malcolm watched as Nikki gave him one last look before she sauntered over to Davis only to strategically slide her arm around his waist, giving him a small peck on his cheek as she glanced back Malcolm's way with a satisfying smile on her face.

Malcolm took a deep dissatisfied breath as he turned to a deadlock stare from Alex. *Fuck.* With all his anger and frustration with Nikki, he forgot to check on Alex. How long had she been watching them? What did she pick up? *Dammit.* They held a stare before Alex broke their invisible connection, turning and walking out onto the patio. *Shit.*

**A**lex stopped short of the rocky waterfall that lined the far side of their pool. She wasn't sure what she saw, just that something didn't seem right: Malcolm and Nikki engaged in what seemed to be a heated conversation of sorts.

It wasn't something that would have normally garnered her attention, but Malcolm was trying way too hard to act like he wasn't talking to her. Unfortunately for him, Alex could tell that they were very much engaged in a conversation. One laced with intimate history.

Alex pushed the frustration through her tight lips, as she glanced over her shoulder to see that Malcolm was talking to another male guest. She turned back around towards the waterfall, the green and blue lights lit up in a collaboration of colors as the water cascaded down the rocky slide and into the open arms of the pool. Alex loved her backyard, so tranquil and calm, the exact opposite of how she felt in this moment. *What in the world could they have been talking about?* Alex thought, turning her eyes to search for Nikki. She watched how she was extra affectionate with Davis and wondered if it was just an act.

Alex's curiosity was piqued, especially given Malcolm's adamant response about *not* knowing her. Her mind began to play devil's advocate, replaying the moments that lead up to Malcolm's last affair, trying to shake off the memory, the pain, the hurt, the broken promises, but they were still there, hanging on her soul like morning dew on fresh cut grass.

The thought of her mom and how her dad hurt her so very much, how she never wanted to be that way, like them. Alex always dreamed of a strong family unit so much that she believed giving someone the benefit of the doubt was not just an option, but a necessity. Alex was willing to do whatever it took to make her marriage work, anything.

A gentle pat on Alex's shoulder pulled her out of her trance as she twirled around to see Lance standing just inches from her.

"Happy birthday, Sis," Lance took a step towards her wrapping his large arms around Alex's medium frame.

"Hey you, so glad you are here." Alex hugged Lance extra tight, hoping some of her frustration would melt away with his assuring touch.

Alex and Lance always had a special relationship. They'd met during Alex's second year of grad school and Lance's first year of undergrad at UCLA. Lance was a freshman on full scholarship and was experiencing a few issues on the field and was assigned to Alex who was in the midst of her internship in the sports psychiatry department. Alex always held a special place in her heart for Lance since he was technically her very first patient even though she wasn't a full-fledged doctor yet, but she treated Lance more like her little brother than a patient. They stayed very close even after Alex and Malcolm started to date which of course led to marriage.

"I wouldn't dare miss this," Lance produced a bottle of wine. "For you. It's the good stuff, a 2008 Nicola Catena Zapata, nothing but the best."

Alex smiled, "Oh no Lance, you didn't have to."

"Come on, now you're just insulting me." They both smiled. Lance turned towards the woman standing next to him, "Alex, this is Vivian Ng, Vivian, this is Dr. Alex Monroe, the birthday girl and my beautiful and amazing sister-in-law."

"Nice to meet you Alex, Lance speaks very highly of you."

"Well that is good to know."

"It's the truth, you are an exquisite woman."

"Okay, you're gonna make it impossible for me to get my head through the door," Alex blushed.

"Please, I only tell you these things because you are modest at best and they are true, but speaking of big heads, where's my brother?"

Alex turned back around only to notice now that Malcolm was talking to another guest; her eyes quickly scanned the room as they landed on Nikki who was still arm and arm with Davis. Alex held her stares between the two looking for nonchalant glances between them, gestures or anything, until...

"Oh, never mind, I see him," Lance interjected. "Let me go holler at him."

"Of course," Alex watched as Lance headed Malcolm's way with his date in tow.

Alex sighed deeply, giving Malcolm one last glance before walking towards the kitchen feeling a tug in her stomach and a sadness in her soul. She wondered how her life would be different if she had not married Malcolm, if she wouldn't have given in to Lance's attempts to set her up with his older brother, a perfect match, he would always say. Alex hated when she played the 'what if' game with herself, second guessing her choices in life that lead her to her here and now. Alex poured herself another glass of wine, took a long sip, as she shook off the negative feelings by throwing a smile on her face.

This was supposed to be her special night, her 40$^{th}$ celebration; Alex took another long sip of her wine before diverting her eyes over towards Malcolm and felt an instinctual pull, something was *not* right. She tried to shake it off, convince herself she was just overreacting, give her husband the benefit of the doubt, and believe that he had indeed changed. Alex took a deep breath as her eyes trailed over to Nikki, who was this woman, this beautiful woman that Malcolm claimed he did not know, but in hindsight was stealing the joy right out from beneath her.

# FIFTEEN

Sylvia couldn't believe her eyes when she saw Lance walking through the door of Alex's birthday party with a *date.* Not less than twelve hours ago he was acting like he wanted her back, acted like he so desperately wanted another shot at proving she was wrong for leaving him. Sylvia scrutinized Lance's interaction with hidden jealously, as they stood just twenty feet away on display in the open concept space of Alex and Malcolm's living room, kitchen and dining room. Sylvia bit the tip of her top lip, shook her head slowly back and forth while contemplating what to say if she found herself forced to converse with them.

"For the record, I told Lance to come alone," Alex's voice floated over Sylvia's shoulders; she turned to see Alex standing behind her.

"And for the record, when has Lance ever listened to anything anyone had to say?" Sylvia said as she swiveled the bar stool towards Alex, "Besides, I am so over that."

"Really?"

"Really," Sylvia repeated in a firm tone. She reached to grab a small white plate with gold trim off of a stack of four and began to fill it with appetizers displayed on the center island.

"I'm sure they're just friends," Alex's eyes drifted over to where Lance and Vivian stood.

"Right and Kim and Kanye are really in love."

Alex smiled at Sylvia's sarcastic, but realistic remark.

"Not to mention, I can't cry over spilled milk."

"Nor should you," Alex reinforced.

"Exactly mama," *especially one as spoiled as Lance*, Sylvia continued her rant in her head considering she knew how close Alex and Lance were. They were all spoiled in her book, all three of them. Although Lance was the most civil of the three she concluded, Malcolm and Lacey had the real issues and it showed in their shitty dispositions.

"Who did your catering? The food is fabulous."

"The same person I always have do it, Seth," Alex said as she reached for the white wine, her gold bangles collapsing together as they slid down her toned arm.

"So is everything else okay?" Alex asked as she placed the bottle back down.

Sylvia looked up from the array of food on her plate, "Yeah, why?"

Alex's left shoulder rose then fell, "I don't know, you seemed kinda emotional earlier, when you were on the patio talking to Malcolm."

"Oh," Sylvia swallowed hard then casually waved her hand in the air, "that... that was nothing, I wasn't emotional, just um, just wasn't feeling well when I first got here, I think it's a bit of jet lag."

"Jet lag?"

"Yes, jet lag. You know how I get when I travel."

"Uh huh," Alex said as she watched Sylvia pile more crackers and cheese on her small but building plate, "we do have bigger plates if needed."

Sylvia stopped, as her eyes took in what Alex was seeing, an embarrassed look spread across her face, "Right, too much?" Sylvia put her plate down, grabbing the sparkling water and pouring it into a wine glass.

"No, it's fine, I've just never seen you eat so much, you're not pregnant are you?"

Sylvia jerked as the water splashed over the rim of the glass, hitting her hand before splashing down onto the white marble countertop, creating a mirrored puddle. She hated how perceptive Alex was, and wondered at times if Alex knew more than what she ever led on.

"Girl please, not in this lifetime," Sylvia gave Alex a quick grin before grabbing a few napkins to catch the cascading water sailing towards the edge of the counter.

"Well you haven't been separated that long and —"

"Nor was I married that long either, so no, Alex, I am *not* pregnant," Sylvia emphasized her last word.

"Okay, although if you were I think that would be the one thing that would make Lance act right."

Sylvia stopped eating and gave Alex an intense stare, "If only it was that easy," Sylvia said.

"You'd be surprised. As long as I've known Lance he has always talked about having kids. I think he would be a great dad."

Sylvia's mind went to what Alex threw out, *Could a baby really make Lance do the right thing??*

"Yeah, I doubt it, seriously, Lance?"

"I'm just saying..." Alex threw out with a raised eyebrow and a friendly smile.

"Alex, please, can we drop the whole pregnancy thing, I am not pregnant," Sylvia said as a wave of nausea washed over her. *Jesus.*

"Fine, sorry," Alex said as she walked closer to Sylvia and leaned against the counter, elbows pressed on the cold stone, hands clasped together, the women were now close in proximity and face to face, "So this Nikki woman, do you know anything more about her?"

Sylvia stopped chewing, felt a chill zigzag through her back, felt her guilt rising a tad.

"No," Sylvia said looking away from Alex's eyes, "Why?"

"I saw her and Malcolm talking."

Sylvia worked to keep her tone calm, she hated lying to her best friend. "It's a party. People talk, don't they?"

"Yeah, I know, but it was the *way* they were talking, ya know? It just seemed... I don't know. I mean, we both know my husband is no saint."

Sylvia began to chew again, slowly, "Right." She was shocked to hear that come out of Alex's mouth, maybe she was waking up to Malcolm's ways after years of turning the other cheek.

"But I just think any woman who knowingly sleeps with another woman's man, let alone a married man, is despicable."

Sylvia felt her mini crab cake swell in her mouth as she attempted to swallow it, she grabbed her water to push it down, past the lump forming in her throat.

"I mean, don't you agree?"

"Yes, of course," Sylvia felt the food that just dropped to her stomach contemplating its return up, "it's definitely not a good look." Sylvia said before she covered her mouth with her left hand, as a gagging sound escaped through her fingers.

"Oh my God, are you okay?" Alex reached out to touch Sylvia's arm.

"Yeah, I um, I shouldn't have eaten that last piece of crab cake, I'm gonna run to the—"

Before Alex had a chance to respond, Sylvia hopped down from the bar stool and headed out the kitchen, down the hall and into the bathroom, where everything she just ate came up. A cold shiver raced through her body. She sat down on the floor, crossing her legs Indian style, feeling sick, frustrated and angry at herself.

She ran her finger through her hair, thought of her friendship with Alex, her failed relationship with Lance and her unwanted pregnancy. Sylvia always knew she was a natural when it came to spinning other people's lives, a task that came with little to no effort, a task that became unattainable when the life suddenly was her own. Sylvia dropped her head, felt the stress of life building in her lower back, fell into deep thought...

It wasn't that her life seemed less than perfect right now that scared her, it was that she had no idea how to fix it or what the hell to do about it.

"Hey, there you are. You okay?" Alex asked, looking Sylvia up and down after she came back from the bathroom.

"Oh, yeah, I'm great. Clearly, I need to lay off the spicy tuna rolls."

Alex's smile flattened into a suspicious grin, "I'm sure."

"Just gonna grab a little ginger ale. You got any?" Sylvia said as she rubbed the back of her neck, feeling the moisture in her hand.

"I think there are a few bottles in the fridge," Alex said. She turned her attention back to the guest she was engaged in conversation with prior to Sylvia re-entering the kitchen.

"Great," Sylvia said before she walked over to the fridge and opened it up, feeling the cool air on her hot body, soaking it in for a second.

Alex and her guest continued to chat as Sylvia noticed them migrating into the living room with their drinks in hand.

She turned her attention back to the open fridge. Scanning the shelves carefully, she finally spotted one bottle of ginger ale on the bottom shelf. She swiped it up feeling the coolness on her palms before placing the bottle against her heated head. She closed the door as she turned on her right foot to notice Lance's date, Vivian, heading her way. *Dammit.*

Without so much as a hello, Sylvia watched as Vivian wondered aimlessly around the kitchen in search for... something. She studied Vivian's body from head to toe in periodic glances. She took in the woman's five foot three frame that flaunted a fitted black dress that delicately snuggled her petite body like a tightly swaddled baby under a light blue cropped jacket. Sylvia scoffed under her breath, *skinny bitch.*

Sylvia rolled her eyes as she managed to throw a welcoming smile on her face and clearing her throat, "If you're looking for drinks, there is a bartender on the patio."

Vivian swung around in an almost animated over-the-top way, "Oh, ha thanks. You must have been reading my mind," Vivian said as she threw her right hand on her hip, "Lance just said go get us some drinks, no kind of direction of any kind. Just about impossible in a house this big. Is it yours?"

Sylvia continued to smile as she devilishly shook her head very inconspicuously, *Where... does he find these women?* "No, actually, this is the birthday girl and her husband's home."

"Of course, duh," Vivian tapped her forehead with her open palm, "Anyway, I'm Vivian Ng, I'm here with Lance, but duh, you know that since I just said he sent me in here. Ha."

"Ha, yes, that was definitely a clue," Sylvia sarcastically matched her tone and energy, then, "I'm Sylvia." She extended her hand out as Vivian stepped in closer to shake it.

Vivian tilted her head to the right as her small eyes got even smaller, "You're a publicist?"

"I am."

"Wait a minute, are you Sylvia Batista?"

"The one and only, yes."

"Oh my gawd, you represent Eva Mendez, I saw you with her in "US" magazine last month."

"Is that right?" Sylvia said as she kept the same sarcastic grin painted on her face.

"Oh you must be good at what you do, Sylvia."

*The comments just don't stop I see.* "I try. And what is it that you do, Vivian?"

"Oh, I'm an intern at ESPN."

*Figures.* "Nice, so I'm assuming that's how you met Lance?"

"Yees, he's so sweet," Vivian cooed.

Sylvia felt an internal roll of her eyes happening before Vivian finished that sentence. "Yeah, he is something," Sylvia continued her smile, tilting her head.

"Oh, do you know him?"

*Oh boy.* Sylvia knew it was only a matter of time and limited small talk before that the question would arise. Her initial thought was to lie. Sylvia knew Lance would die if he knew she and Vivian were even engaged in a conversation right now, then again, he shouldn't let his dates roam around without supervision.

"Know… who?" Sylvia threw out, buying time, contemplating if she should tell Vivian the truth or if it would make her uncomfortable.

"Lance, how do you two know each other?"

"Oh, we are… um," Sylvia clears her throat, "married but--"

"What? You're married?"

"Separated, separated," Sylvia corrected her Freudian slip, "you didn't let me finish."

"Oh my God, you're... his... wife?" Vivian said as her eyes began to grow larger by the second as she processed the information.

"Technically speaking, yes, but equivocally speaking, no, that is as soon as he signs the divorce papers,"

"Oh my god, what's happening?" Vivian did a quick scan of Sylvia's body, "Lance never said he was *ever* married."

*Shocking.* "Really? Well I'm sure it just slipped his mind."

"And now I am finding out he was married to you, Sylvia Batista?" Vivian said with a stiff tone. Sylvia wasn't sure if that was a compliment or a dig... either way she wasn't going to challenge it.

Vivian broke out in a nervous laugh. "I mean how do you come after Sylvia Batista, right?"

"Riiight." Maybe telling Vivian she was Lance's soon-to-be ex-wife wasn't such a grand idea after all. Sylvia looked around for Lance, because it was official, this was getting weird. She finally spotted him in the far corner talking to Malcolm.

Sylvia stepped back a few inches, "Well it was so nice to meet you Vivian, I'm sure Lance is waiting for that drink." Sylvia pointed past Vivian towards Lance, "I think I see him right over there."

Vivian turned to look in that direction before turning back towards Sylvia, she now had a weird glare in her eye, "You're right, I should go." Vivian gave Sylvia a half-smile before she turned and walked out of the kitchen.

"Jesus," Sylvia kinda laughed to herself as she watched Vivian approach Lance, her mouth moving a mile a minute. Lance looked annoyed, very annoyed as he turned to find the source of Vivian's demise.

Sylvia turned away picking up her ginger ale, taking a huge gulp as if she was in her own world. She placed the bottle down as a satisfying grin did a happy dance across her face. For the first time today, she was starting to feel a lot better.

# SIXTEEN

Lacey sipped her third glass of wine, keeping a close eye on Reagan. Lacey hated how she couldn't stop starring at her as the night progressed.

From the first moment Lacey laid eyes on Reagan she'd felt an instant attraction to her. It was a foreign feeling that her mind fought to combat, but her emotions finally won over. It wasn't just her tall lean body, evidence of years of Pilates, or her long wavy hair the color of a perfectly made caramel latte that complemented her natural skin like the outside of a ginger root, it was her whole being, the energy that she possessed and ultimately their undeniable chemistry.

Lacey took another sip from her glass as she pushed frustration and desire through her parted lips and caged thoughts, *Why did she have to look so damn sexy? Why is she even here in LA? She wasn't supposed to be back until next month!* Faint memories were washing up in her mind like waves on a sandy beach. The alcohol began whispering the types of things in her ear that she shouldn't be thinking. Lacey glanced around the party in progress only to have her eyes wander back to Reagan like an obedient boomerang.

Lacey scanned Reagan's face, then hair, taking in her full lips, fine nose and beautiful brown curly hair. Reagan never wore a lot of make-up, she was what you would call a natural beauty, something that drove Lacey crazy, and it was something that made Reagan even more alluring.

She looked away then back again only this time to be met with Reagan's returned stare.

*Shit,* Lacey looked down then back up. Their eyes locked as Lacey felt a warm sensation dance between her legs. She smiled then glanced away again as she took another sip of her white wine which was now in need of a refill.

"Maybe you should slow down a bit." Randolph's voice startled Lacey pulling her thoughts away from Reagan and onto him.

Lacey looked down at her glass that was a quarter full, "This is my second glass."

"Third, if you are anticipating another trip to the bar."

"Really, so now you are monitoring my wine intake?"

Randolph gave Lacey a patronizing smile, he didn't want to fight, "Maybe we should call it a night sweetheart…."

*Maybe you should call it a night,* Lacey thought to herself taking one last swig from her glass, finishing off what was left. She shot another quick glance Reagan's way. "I'm not ready to go, not yet."

"It's getting late. I should get our coats." Randolph turned to complete his mission, but Lacey placed her hand gently on his. She dropped her head and her voice and went into baby mode.

"Sweetie, let's stay just a little longer. I haven't seen my family in so long," Lacey said in her sweetest voice ever.

Randolph looked a bit annoyed but tried to be understanding. He tapped his hand against his leg, processing the information, "Fine, we can stay a bit longer, but I do have an early morning, so not too much longer."

Lacey knew she was a master at getting what she wanted and she did it well, "Great, let's dance. I love this song," Lacey said. She began to groove, running her hands up and down his arm, shooting Reagan a sidelong glance. Lacey now noticed Reagan was watching their every move which made her become that much more aggressive with Randolph for him to dance with her.

"Lacey, you know I don't like to dance," Randolph said with an annoyed tone.

"I just thought maybe this one time you..." realizing she shouldn't push it, "Fine, you're right, I shouldn't force you to do anything you don't want to do."

"Thank you."

Lacey then noticed Reagan heading towards the back of the house.

"I'll be right back."

"Where are you going?"

Lacey searched for the most convincing lie, "Ladies room. Is that gonna be a problem too?"

Randolph smiled as he reached both his hands out making contact with Lacey's shoulders, "Don't be silly, of course not. I'll be right here when you get back," he said as he slowly slid his hands down the side of her arms with equal pace.

Lacey stepped back as Randolph's hands fell off her, "Perfect."

Lacey set her empty glass down on the cocktail table and headed in the direction where she saw Reagan go. As Lacey turned the corner and out of eye sight of Randolph, she hoped he didn't pick up on her true destination.

Reagan entered the bathroom, shutting the door behind her, *yep, this is gonna be harder than she thought,* Reagan said to herself as she leaned against the vanity and stared at her caramel-colored face in the reflection. She shouldn't have come, she knew she would feel this way.

She knew seeing Lacey would manifest feelings she wasn't ready to deal with. Reagan closed her eyes trying to block out what she was feeling, trying to remember what went down before she left for her trip, realizing the motivation behind the trip was to separate herself from Lacey, to clear her mind, forget about what they had shared. She looked up and was startled to see Lacey walking through the bathroom door, closing it softly behind her, locking it firmly.

"Hey there sexy..." Lacey leaned against the door.

Reagan rolled her eyes and shook her head; some things never change, "You're drunk."

"And *you* are very observant. One thing I love about you."

Reagan felt Lacey's eyes roam over her, a clean and ravenous glance that would have alarmed Reagan if she wasn't used to it.

As a lesbian, Reagan always knew how to spot the bi-curious women. It was in their eyes and how they looked at her, how they interacted. Most of them fantasized about being with a woman, but few acted upon it. The ones that didn't have their own internal battles and crosses to bear. Then there were the ones who teetered on that thin line only to fall over to the other side, to later regret their actions brought on by too much tequila. Lacey acted on her urges, but now in perfect Lacey fashion, she didn't know how to let it go.

Reagan knew getting involved with a woman conflicted about her sexuality was a one way ticket to nowhere, but there was something about Lacey that she couldn't resist and still couldn't.

"So now you follow people into bathrooms."

"Just you…" Lacey said licking her lips then smiling.

Reagan shook her head, *I so do not have time for this, not now.* "What do you want Lace?"

Lacey raised an eyebrow as she twirled the side of her hair, "I just wanted to talk, that's all."

"We've been at this party for two hours now, you couldn't find the time then?"

"Maybe I needed to talk to you… alone."

"Right, alone. God forbid your "fiancé" sees you talking to your ex-lover. Are you afraid he will see right through your charade?"

"It's not like that…really."

"Then what is it?" Reagan asked, in a tone that screamed she was over this.

Lacey paused, looked down and back up, "I didn't come here to fight."

"Then why did you come in here?"

"I want it to be like it was, before you left."

"Lacey that's impossible because we want two different things."

"I don't understand why you had to make such a big deal about it. Why it had to be so official. We used to have so much fun," Lacey began to rub her hands down the front of her, "and the sex, my gawd, I miss that with you, the way you used to —"

"It wasn't about the sex for me, Lace."

"Seriously? You didn't like our sex?"

Reagan shook her head, "You're missing the point. That's not who I am anymore Lace, yes the sex was... amazing, but I can't continue living in the closet. Living a lie. I'm out now and I'm happy, you should try it."

Lacey shook her head slowly, "Yeah...you know I can't do that."

"Can't or won't?"

Lacey tossed her arms up in frustration, "God, what is wrong with you? What was so wrong with what we had?"

"What we had was a lie, Lace. You know it and I know it. I don't want to live my life on the DL... I'm done with that."

"So you're done with me?"

Reagan felt a pulsing sensation in her neck. *No*. "Yes."

Lacey looked away as Reagan watched her process what she just said, then back up at her, "Reagan... I have fans now, I have an image to uphold."

Reagan stared at Lacey for a second before letting out a loud forceful laugh. *Really? How much more frustrating can this get?* "Well God forbid they know you like women. What would the world think?"

"That's something I am not willing to find out."

"Then you're not willing to be with me."

"I'm not like you. My family, my fans, they would never understand, not in a million years."

"Don't forget your fiancé..." Reagan said, feeling a tinge of jealousy at the mere mention of Lacey's new lover in her life.

"Reagan, my career is just now taking off. I can't jeopardize it, not now."

"Then when?"

Lacey and Reagan hold a stare, "I don't know."

Reagan was tired of playing these games, so done with it, "Lace I came out thinking we would be together and you took a big ass step back, leaving me all alone."

"I'm sorry but...this just isn't me—"

"And marrying a pastor is, what are you trying to prove here?"

"Nothing!"

"Then what are you doing?" Reagan said feeling as if she was pleading for Lacey to finally just finally admit her true feelings. .

"I'm just trying to do the right thing."

"For you or for the opinions of others, because you can't live your life for anyone else but yourself."

An awkward silence fell between them. Lacey looked down shaking her head from side to side. Reagan knew she hit a cord with Lacey, she knew this wasn't what she wanted to hear, she knew Reagan was right but was too scared to admit it.

"Clearly this was a mistake coming in here." Lacey said as she shifted in her place.

"Yes, I think it was."

Lacey finally looked up, "Wow..." Lacey wiped a tear from her face. "So this is it, huh?"

Reagan felt her heart crumbling into tiny little pieces. She always knew getting involved with Lacey would eventually lead to angst and pain, but she couldn't make a person be who they truly desired if they were too scared to take that chance.

Reagan looked into Lacey eyes. "Looks that way."

Lacey opened her mouth before pushing out a smile, "Okay, I um, if that's what you really want."

"No Lace, it's what you want."

Silence fell between them, and a knock on the door startled them, "Will be done in a minute," Reagan yelled back.

"I guess I better get back... to my fiancé."

"Yep, good luck with your new life," Reagan said then turned back towards the mirror and stared at her own reflection.

Lacey turned to leave. The moment the door closed, tears that she had forced back came streaming down her face.

# SEVENTEEN

"Hi, can I talk to you for a second?" Lance wasn't waiting for an answer as he gently pulled Sylvia by the arm to a secluded area of the house.

"Well hello to you too. I didn't see you come in."

Lance just smiled, and folded his arms in front of his chest, "Didn't see me come in huh?"

Sylvia watched while Lance kept a small grin on his face. He was definitely going somewhere with this, where she had no idea. But she was curious to see where he was taking it.

"Ah, nope, sure didn't," Sylvia said as she admired Lance's crisp black shirt under his grey blazer and dark blue True Religion jeans. He was always so well put together. Tonight was no different.

"So I guess if you didn't see me come in, you didn't see the woman that came in with me either?"

Sylvia knew Lance could tell she was lying, but why confirm his suspicions? Or make it easy for him?

"Ah, no, I… did not."

Lance unfolded his arms and dropped them down to his waist sliding them into his pants pockets, then tilting his head to the right, "Sylvia, cut the crap please, I saw you talking to Vivian."

Sylvia's blossoming smile spread across her face, "Oh, is that her name? Vivian. Well just so you know, this party is for family and friends, not underage jump offs."

Lance threw his head back as a loud chuckle fell out of his mouth, "Now *that* is funny. And just so we're clear, Vivian is 25 and we are just friends."

"Ah, 25, don't you have a collection of wine older than her?"

Lance chuckled again, nodding his head up and down, "I like it when you get jealous. Lets me know I still have a chance with you," Lance threw out, testing the rocky waters known as Sylvia Batista.

Sylvia stared at the arrogance plastered all over Lance's face, "Yeah, I doubt that."

Lance took a small step towards her, dropped his voice down to a whisper, "It doesn't make you jealous when I am with other women?"

Lance didn't wait for a response as his eyebrow arched up, "I think it does."

Sylvia felt her body grow warm from Lance's statement. She hated how well he knew her. She especially hated the fact his 25-year-old jump off did make her jealous. But the last thing she would ever do was give him the satisfaction of knowing that.

Lance leaned in a wee bit closer, "I think it makes you batshit crazy."

A loud hiss blew through her lips as she shook her head and kept her eyes planted on Lance, "I think you're dreaming and I think you need to take a few steps back out of my personal space before your *jump off*… I mean your *friend* sees you misbehaving."

Lance reached up and scratched the side of his face, "Well see that's the problem, *and* the reason we are conversing in this moment. Vivian, the woman I came with to the party, just left."

*Great*, Sylvia thought as she fought hard, mighty hard to keep that smile she had from bursting through.

"She did?" Sylvia said, attempting to put on her shocked face.

"Yes, she did, and in my car."

*Even better,* Sylvia continued with her inner dialogue as she looked around the party then back at Lance. "Why is she driving your car?" Sylvia couldn't help hide her sneering grin before finishing her thought out loud, "Oh right, that nasty DUI."

Lance cut his eyes to the right, as he shook his head in the memory. "Yeah, that."

"Well do you think she's coming back for you? Because I would love to give you a ride but you live in Malibu and I live in Westwood and well just thinking of backtracking on the 405 is—"

"I'm not asking you for a ride home, Sylvia, I am asking what you said to her," Lance said, intentionally locking his eyes on Sylvia, patiently waiting for her response.

Sylvia swallowed, felt the nausea stirring again in her belly, and wondered what he might say if she told him the truth. What would really happen if she told him that she scared the skinny bitch off so she could talk to him alone and tell him that she was pregnant with his child?

Instead, what came out was, "Nothing, we were just having girl talk, that's what girls do," Sylvia said. She realized that she needed to walk away from Lance before she threw up all over his Martin Dingman leather shoes. She was about to act on that urge, but Lance had a different thought as he blocked her way.

"Oh no, no, no. You said something, because *she* is gone, so *you* are going to tell me what happened."

"Why does it matter? She's just a friend, right?" Sylvia said, as she looked away, avoiding all eye contact with Lance. She wanted very badly for this conversation to be over before it took a very wrong turn.

"Wait, you told her we were married, didn't you?"

Sylvia could feel Lance searching for eye contact, for confirmation of his statement.

"Sylvia?"

*Shit*. Sylvia finally looked up, their eyes entangled in a tug of war then, "Okay, but I didn't volunteer the information. She asked, I confirmed."

Lance threw up his arms, "Unbelievable. Why would you do that?"

"I don't know, maybe because we are?"

"I wouldn't call being married for 3 months a marriage."

"And whose fault was that?" Sylvia shot back.

Lance turned away, massaged his own temples with his thumb and fore finger before he swung back around to face Sylvia, "I was NOT the one who wanted the divorce, Sylvia, you did."

"Yeah, you damn right I did, after the way you treated me just weeks after our wedding, who wouldn't?"

Sylvia saw Lance's jaw tighten as the muscle on the side of his cheek began to bulge out, "I told you what happened."

"You told me what you wanted me to hear."

"Which was the truth."

"Well… that was questionable," Sylvia said as she felt her body begin to quiver from the residual roller coaster Lance put her through. "Everything you do is questionable and that is why we will never be together Lance." Sylvia hoped he didn't see how badly she was shaking. She really hoped that he didn't see right through the lie.

Sylvia tried to walk past Lance once again but he grabbed her by the arm and pulled her into him. "The more you deny it, the more I know you want me."

Sylvia scoffed, "If that is what gets you through the night… keep dreaming."

"You threw our marriage in her face to get rid of her. I know you Sylvia, you act like you don't want me, but I know you do."

"Let me go," Sylvia said as she tried to pull from Lance's iron clad grip.

Lance ignored her plea, "It's only a matter of time before you realize that we belong together."

"Stop it."

He pulled her in closer, then leaned down and whispered in her ear, "I know you miss me and I know you miss that thing I used to do? Tell me you don't…"

Sylvia felt a throbbing sensation leap between her legs as her body language remained unaltered, her face unresponsive. Lance dropped his hand down to Sylvia's hips and around to her ass, pulling her against his erect penis. Sylvia let out a short gasp.

"Tell me," Lance repeated.

Sylvia couldn't let herself slip back into his clutches, not this way, not now, she swallowed hard, "Let me go, now," Sylvia gave Lance a stern look.

They stared at each other, neither one wanting to give an inch. Finally, Lance released Sylvia's arm.

"Fine," Lance said.

Sylvia took a deep breath as she turned and started to walk away from Lance when she heard, "Just answer me one question."

Sylvia stopped, as she squeezed her eyes shut tight, not looking back, not wanting to hear what was next, "What?"

"Why do you keep doing this?"

"Doing what?" Sylvia turned to see a more serious look on Lance's face.

"Pushing me away, I told you I fucked up, I told you it would never happen again. Why won't you give me another chance?"

"Because your word isn't good enough."

"How so?"

"Because you also told me you would get help and here we are a year later, with a court case and a possible criminal record. So you tell me, when will it end Lance?"

Lance dropped his head, shaking it from side to side before looking back up at Sylvia, "It's not that simple."

"Well, it's not that hard either."

"It's not what you think!" Lance protested.

Sylvia stepped closer to him, "Then what is it? Why can't you talk to me?"

For the first time Lance was at a loss for words, he shrugged his shoulders, "You wouldn't understand."

"Try me."

Sylvia knew there was a lot that Lance didn't share with her about his life, about his childhood, about how he'd become a man. She wanted so badly to help him, but he continued to shut her down and shut her out. One of the reasons she knew for sure that she could not have this baby with him, not with so many unanswered questions.

Lance and Sylvia held another long, intense stare. Lance retreated, and took a deep breath.

"Listen, sorry for stepping to you about Vivian, it um, it won't happen again, promise," Lance said as he turned to walk away.

"So you're gonna do what Lance does best huh? Just walk away and shut it down?"

Lance didn't acknowledge what Sylvia said as he continued to walk away.

"One day, you have to talk about it, you can't keep running from it Lance," she called after him.

As Lance disappeared to the other room, Sylvia shook her head, as she rubbed her stomach.

# EIGHTEEN

"So what were you and Nikki talking about?" Alex's voice was low while she kept a pleasant smile on her face. She braced herself for the worst; she knew her husband was no saint, she knew that at any moment she could find out there was another woman in his life, another betrayal.

Malcolm stopped in his tracks as he turned to face Alex with a complex look scribbled all over his face. "Who?"

"Nikki. Davis's date. I saw you two talking."

Malcolm stepped out into the backyard, took a few more steps before turning and facing Alex once again, "Babe it's a party, people talk. Are you really asking me this right now?"

Alex didn't feel like having this conversation either, but she knew something wasn't right and she had to get to the bottom of it, now, "Yes, I am Malcolm because from where I was standing it looked… weird."

"Weird?"

"Yes, personal, as in you two already knew each other…" Alex took a deep breath, bracing herself. "So do you?"

"Do I what Alex?" Malcolm's annoyed look only grew more intense.

Alex felt her frustration building as she worked overtime to keep it concealed, "Do you already know her?" she said with a forceful tone.

Malcolm shifted, rubbed the side of his face, "I told you, I've never seen her before, okay?"

Alex looked down, felt a knot growing in her throat reaching all the way down to her stomach. *Something still didn't feel right.* She had to go one step further, ask what was on her heart, deep in her soul, laced with intuition.

She held her breath, then released, "Are you having another affair, Malcolm?"

"Oh my God," Malcolm laughed out loud. "Seriously Alex, are we going there again?" Malcolm's last few words were loud, too loud.

"Would you please keep your voice down?" Alex said, noticing a few of her guests' heads turn in response to Malcolm's mini-outburst. Alex smiled politely at them and then gestured to Malcolm.

They moved past a few of their guests as they walked out onto the patio next to the swimming pool making sure they were out of earshot of everyone.

"Then why did you bring it up now? Huh? In the middle of your party?"

"I don't know, something in me moved me to ask. Call it woman's intuition."

"Well your intuition is wrong."

"Is it Malcolm, I mean you two just seemed —"

Malcolm put his hand up, "Listen, Alex, if you really want to know, she was asking me if I could read a script she wrote and you know how much I hate that shit, okay? That was the beginning, middle and the end of our conversation. Babe, you are reading too much into it, seriously, just relax."

Alex opened her mouth to say something but stopped. Maybe Malcolm was right, maybe she was jumping to conclusions. Maybe she was trying to see something that wasn't true."

"Babe, I'm not having an affair, okay?"

Alex was silent.

Malcolm repeated himself for clarity, "Okay?"

Alex sighed, "Okay, I'm sorry, I just… I'm just—"

Malcolm caressed the side of Alex's face, "I know, it's a big day for you, a lot going on. Can we just enjoy the party, please? Matter of fact…" Malcolm turned and grabbed a drink from a passing waiter. He reached over to one of the high tables to grab a spoon and tap lightly to get everyone's attention.

"Can I get everyone's attention please?" Malcolm looked at Alex and then out into the eyes of her dozen or so guests that were gathering around them. Some of the inside guests were now slowly making their way outside. A hush fell over the small crowd.

"Thanks… Um… I just wanted to take a moment to say thank you to everyone who came out tonight to celebrate Alex's 40th birthday. It means a lot to me and I am sure to Alex as well, to have our closest friends here to celebrate this night with us." Malcolm raised an eyebrow, "Especially since most of you know I don't like too many folks up in Casa De Monroe."

The room filled with laughter as Malcolm lifted his glass.

"Also," Alex added "I know it is my birthday celebration but I just wanted to take a moment to recognize my father-in-law Langston Monroe. 20 years ago, tomorrow, a great man was lost and although he is gone he will never be forgotten. He was a great man who in hindsight produced not only great music but this great man standing in front of me, my husband."

Alex turned to look at Malcolm as he gave Alex a small smile, then lifted up his glass. "To my dad, but mostly to my beautiful wife, may this day bring you joy, happiness and everything your heart desires. I love you babe and I hope to grow old and feeble with you. Cheers."

Everyone in the room followed suit, their glasses clinking as guests toasted the couple.

Alex felt her body relaxing a bit, as Malcolm leaned in and planted a soft kiss on her cheek. Alex produced a smile on her solemn face as she scanned her birthday crowd, but also couldn't help to look in the direction of Nikki, then back at Malcolm.

"So please, eat, drink, and be merry, but at midnight, ya gotta go," Malcolm joked as everyone laughed again before they returned to mingling.

"That was a very sweet toast." Alex turned towards Malcolm.

"I just said what was on my heart. You know I love you and I know I can be a bit of an ass, but my heart still belongs to you."

Alex took a step toward Malcolm as she wrapped her arms around his neck, "I love you too. You may just get lucky later." Alex went in for a seductive kiss on his lips.

"That was my plan the whole time, ya know?"

"Is that right?" Alex gave a knowing smile, "well your plan just may have worked Mr. Monroe." Alex and Malcolm shared another kiss and for the first time she felt as if they were on the same page.

"Oh, I almost forgot," Malcolm dug into his pocket and pulled out a small gift box, "Happy Birthday." Malcolm handed Alex her gift. Alex smiled as she already knew what was laying inside, the one carat diamond earrings.

"Awww, thank you honey." Alex pressed her lips softly against Malcolm's lips then opened the box to reveal a pair of diamond hoops.

Alex stared at the hoops, and wasn't sure if this was a joke or her reality, *what is going on, where are the diamond studs she saw upstairs in his pocket?*

"You don't like them?"

Alex looked up, didn't know what to say, didn't know how to feel, "Yeah, I um, I love them."

"You're always saying how you wanted some diamond hoops, right?"

"Right... I did," Alex stared at the hoops she held in her hand, trying not to snap off in that moment, trying to digest the fact that the diamond earrings she saw in Malcolm's pocket were not for her, then who?

Alex looked over Malcolm's shoulder to see her boss, Dr. Blackwell, coming her way. She quickly threw a warm smile on her face, then looking up at Malcolm, "Thank you, I love them."

"Cool, I knew you would."

"There you are," Dr. Blackwell said beaming Alex's way.

"Well hello Dan, you made it," Alex said as she gave her boss a friendly hug.

"Where is your wife?"

"Our son came down with a fever and we couldn't get a babysitter at the last minute, but she wanted me to tell you happy birthday and she would love to take you to lunch next week."

"Tell her it's a date. Dan you remember my husband, Malcolm, right?"

"I certainly do, it is great to see you again, Malcolm."

"Same here, Doctor, same here."

"Please, call me Dan. Great toast by the way, I caught the tail end of it. Alex has trained you well."

Malcolm laughed, "Yes she has. You know what they say, happy wife happy life."

"Very true, indeed, so I am sure her new position in San Francisco will make the wife even happier."

*Holy shit.* Alex froze, felt as if the floor dropped out from under her, she *did not* expect Dan to mention her possible promotion and position to Malcolm without a final consult with her.

"Excuse me? What move Dan?" Malcolm questioned.

Dan gave Alex a confused look before stuttering out, "Um…."

Alex swallowed hard past the lump in her throat, "Dan, I didn't get a chance to discuss with Malcolm about that yet, with the party and all—"

"So what's this new position, Alex?" Malcolm asked, a serious look suddenly on his face.

Alex knew this was not the time to discuss this, not with a house full of guests, "Babe, we can talk about it later."

"No, I think we need to talk about it now."

"Actually Malcolm nothing is really set in stone, here, it's just an option," Dan said, trying to do his best to soften the bomb he just dropped on them.

Alex looked at her boss, "It's okay Dan."

She turned to her husband who was quietly fuming, "I was gonna talk to you about this but with the party and the—".

"Well let's hear it now, I am all ears Alex, all ears," Malcolm said as he cupped both of his ears with the palm of his hands.

"Don't do this, Malcolm, not now."

"What? I would love to hear this fantastic news that was not told to me by my wife."

Alex bit down on her lip, she knew Malcolm would not stop until he was satisfied, "Fine," Alex shot Dan a look before focusing on Malcolm, "A position opened up with the 49ers and I think this would be an amazing opportunity for not just me but for you too."

"For us?" Malcolm looked at Dan, "Now isn't that sweet, my wife has decided to take a position outside of LA without even consulting me on it, but it's a great opportunity for us."

Alex felt the urge to scream and cry, but she didn't, not in front of her guest, "I don't even have the job."

"But you are considering it, correct?"

Alex was silent.

Malcolm shook his head, "You know what Alex it's good that you are quiet because I've heard just about enough. Once again it's 'Fuck Malcolm's career' huh…?" He stormed off ignoring Alex's crushed look.

Dan reached out and softly touched Alex's arm, "Alex I'm sorry, I thought you—"

Alex put up her hand, "It's okay Dan. It's not your fault, really. I just need to go talk to him, everything will be fine."

"Of course."

Alex headed in the direction behind Malcolm as she noticed the sympathetic eyes of her guests falling on her, she ignored them and continued on her way calling behind Malcolm, "Can you just wait a minute, please?"

Malcolm didn't acknowledge Alex and kept walking. He stormed to the back of the house, into their theater room, shutting the door behind him.

Alex stopped just before the door, took a deep breath and opened the door.

"Babe, come on, I tried to talk to you about this earlier but you didn't want to talk."

Alex watched as Malcolm paced back and forth, before stopping and looking her dead in her eyes, "I cannot *believe* you would even consider taking a job in the Bay Area."

"I know it's a big move, but it's a great opportunity."

"For the love of God, stop saying how great this fucking opportunity is, because the way I look at it it's not."

Malcolm cupped his hand behind his head as he continued to pace, "And what am I supposed to do about my career? Huh? I need to be in LA."

"You're a filmmaker, you can live anywhere, that's the beauty of your job," Alex pleaded with him as she took a few steps closer to Malcolm, trying to make him see this through another angle.

"Is that your way of lessening your guilt? Or to try and sway me to move? Because I am not moving Alex. Period."

"No, I am just thinking how we can compromise here. If you look at the bigger picture, it could work, especially now that you have your distribution deal. Your film will be released and afterwards you can focus on writing your next project. You don't have to be in LA to write, babe."

Malcolm let out a huge grunt, dropping his hands to the side. "Fuck, I cannot do this."

Malcolm sat down on the edge of one of their plush recliners that faced the six foot screen, head dropped into the palm of his hands.

"Babe, it can work," Alex reassured him.

"No it can't Alex," Malcolm stood again.

"Can we at least try?" Alex continued to plead.

"I said no."

"Why not?"

"Because I didn't get that distribution deal," Malcolm yelled back.

Alex froze, she couldn't believe what just came out of Malcolm's mouth. She wondered if she'd even heard him correctly, "What? But you said—"

"I know what the fuck I said, okay?"

Alex shook her head, *this is not happening*, "Why did you lie?"

"Why did I lie?" Malcolm turned to face Alex, as he let out a hurtful laugh, "I lied because I didn't want to see *that* look on your face one more *goddamn* time, that's why, that look of fucking pity and disappointment and frustration. That's why I lied."

Alex swallowed hard, raked her fingers through her short hair, "Well, what happened? How could they not give it to you? I mean—"

Malcolm looked up at her, his eyes narrowed and darkened, "Is that all you have to say? Really?"

"What am I supposed to say?" Alex yelled back this time.

"Say you understand my pain. Say you know it will get better. Say something that's not a fucking question."

"I don't know what to say to you anymore. I'm trying my best to be there for you but you keep pushing me away."

"So it's my fault?" Malcolm said as he walked away from Alex.

"It's no one's fault, we just have to figure out a way to make it work…"

Malcolm swung back around, "How Alex? By you deciding to take a job in San Francisco without even considering me? Or how it would affect me?"

"I always consider you. Always. Maybe it's time for you to start considering me."

Malcolm's face scrunched up, "And what is that supposed to mean?"

"You promised that we would have children and we are still childless."

"Now is just not the right time."

"Hello? I'm forty years old Malcolm, it's now or never."

"I told you I need some time, we can't afford a baby now."

"With this new position, we can. My salary will double, don't you see? With that, we can do so much more."

"No Alex, *you* can do so much more," Malcolm headed for the door. "It's not like it used to be Alex, my trust fund is gone. All I have left is this stupid house."

"Can we just talk about this later? We have a house full of guests."

"You know what Alex…? No, we can't talk about this later, I'm done talking."

Malcolm opened the door before storming out and slamming it behind him.

"Malcolm," Alex called through the closed door. Hearing nothing in return, she looked around the lavish theater room with plush furniture and state-of-the-art equipment and knew that in that moment nothing was more important than the sound of Malcolm's voice.

# NINETEEN

Malcolm hit a switch and light flooded into the 1,000 square foot game room. A large pool table sat in the far right side of the room across from a full bar and a large 50-inch television screen, with a black leather sectional with deep cushions was perched in front of it, this was definitely Malcolm's man cave. A much-needed place to come and retreat.

Malcolm walked behind the bar, grabbed the nearest bottle of Jack Daniels, pulled a glass from the above rack and poured until the glass was half full.

He took a large gulp and quickly replenished his glass. He lifted the glass to his lips, and stopped, as if contemplating his next move. He slowly placed the full glass back down and reached under the bar to grab a hidden electronic cigarette. Taking a few drags he closed his eyes then opened them as he put the cigarette down on the bar as he picked up his glass of Jack, tossing the brown liquid down his throat.

Malcolm stood, feeling a wave of relief flow through his body. He raked his fingers through his short twist before walking over to the red top pool table. That sat as the focal point of the room.

Grabbing a two-toned pool stick from the wall, he retrieved the white ball from under the table, eyeing the twenty four balls in the set position on the far end of the bright red tarmac. He leaned over, placing the white ball front and center.

Malcolm took one last gulp of his Jack and set the glass down on the black rubbery rim before grabbing his electronic pleasure, pulling in a few drags and setting it down next to the glass. He leaned over to get a good view of his target before extending his right arm back like a sling shot, quickly shooting forward and slamming the brown two-toned stick against the white ball. *Clack.*

Malcolm watched the white ball shoot across the table and collide with the others, the thunderous sound filling the room as the colored balls scattered across the table.

Just that bit of force from the pool stick helped release a fragment of stress from Malcolm's body, but he needed more, much more. Malcolm bent over to repeat what he had just done when he heard...

"You never were consistent on the table."

Malcolm looked up to see his brother Lance standing in the doorway.

"Like you can talk," Malcolm leaned over, taking another shot. *Clack.* And again, failing to sink a ball.

Lance shook his head, then walked closer to where Malcolm stood, "I see you're smoking again."

Malcolm glanced down at his electronic cigarette that laid beside his empty glass, then back up at his brother, "Don't you know, this is the healthy alternative."

Lance chuckled, "Healthy until Alex finds out."

"Yeah, well that won't happen," Malcolm said as he pulled two equal drags from it then tucking it away in his pants pocket.

"That was quite the scene back there," Lance said as he took a few more steps towards Malcolm.

"I'm glad you enjoyed it," Malcolm replied sullenly.

"Just so you know, your walls are not sound proof when you're yelling."

"Thanks for that tip," Malcolm threw back.

"But hey, what's a house party without a little drama, right?" Lance threw out.

"Yeah, you would know."

Lance gave a small smile. "Touché my brother, touché." Lance walked over to the bar, poured himself a shot of vodka, then a second, then a third, throwing them back one after the other.

"I see you're taking that DUI with a grain of salt. Something you want to talk about?"

"Nah, it's under control," Lance said as he grabbed a pool stick, chalking it and leaned over the table to take a shot immediately sinking the blue solid ball, "I guess I'm solids," Lance said shrugging his shoulders with a satisfying "don't hate" grin.

Malcolm frowned as he watched Lance sink solid ball after solid ball running the table before standing and looking up at Malcolm, "So what's up? What's really going on with you and Alex?"

Malcolm took a sip from his glass, "Nothing man…" He bent over to shoot a striped ball in the far left pocket, which he missed. "Son of a bitch."

"Didn't seem like nothing up there," Lance positioned his stick to take another shot and looked up, "You may as well tell me because you know Alex will eventually." Lance eyed his intended target with one eye closed.

Malcolm took a deep breath, "Alex got a job opportunity with the 49ers."

Lance stopped mid-shot and stood, "Dude, that's tight."

"No asshole, it's not *tight*, I'm not moving up to the bay."

"Why the fuck not?" Lance threw back.

"Because I need to be in LA, that's why!"

"So, this is like, a promotion?" Lance bent over and quickly sank another solid in the middle pocket.

Malcolm shrugged his shoulders, "I don't know what it is, and really don't care."

"Well I say you go, try it out. Not like you *really* have to be in LA."

Malcolm threw his stick on the table, "What the hell am I going to do up there?"

"The same thing you doing down here, a whole lot of nothing."

"You know what? Fuck you man." Malcolm walked over to the bar and grabbed a beer from the fridge.

Lance laughed, "So now you're mad at me?"

"You always fucking siding with her."

"Because she's always right. Dude, it's clear as fucking day she makes more money than you—"

"I don't care about that."

"Yeah you do, because with money comes power and with power there's control and that's why you are down here in this cave pouting because you like to be in control, and right now you ain't."

"Man please, you need to go somewhere with that, you over here telling me how I'm living and you can't even stay married?"

"True, but Sylvia and I are working on it."

"Working on what?"

"Us."

Malcolm shook his head, as a loud chuckle escaped through his lips, "You need to leave her alone. I told you not to marry her from the jump."

"Like I'm going to listen to you."

"And look where that got you. Fucking divorced."

"At least I can admit that I was wrong, maybe you need to take a note from that book."

Malcolm laughed again, a bit more nonchalant, "Yeah, well don't hold your breath."

"I don't have to be married to know how to compromise, and you have no clue as to what that is."

"I forgot you were such a fucking pro."

"I didn't say I was a pro."

"Then what are you saying?"

"That Alex has been putting up with your shit for years, this can't be the first time she turned down a better gig for you, when are you gonna get it?"

"Get what?"

"That Alex is the bread winner, yo, and you go where the bread is being offered."

"Please… In her dreams…"

"In her dreams? What do you have Malcolm? Because the last time I looked around our family was broke, okay?"

"It's gone for now, but I'm getting our money back."

"Yo, when are you gonna get it through your head? That money is gone, the bank account, the trust funds, gone. It's been twenty years Malcolm… that money is not gonna magically materialize back into our pockets, okay? Wake up and face the fact that Dad had shady motherfuckers working for him and they took all that shit, not giving a shit about his three kids or wife. We're lucky we even have this house and his platinum records to show for all he did."

Malcolm stood quiet, not wanting to face reality, even after twenty years of denial. His life wasn't supposed to turn out like this, struggle after struggle. He knew his family was broke even if the world thought differently. This was a pill he'd been trying to swallow for the last twenty years, but couldn't.

Malcolm picked up his pool stick, bending over and sinking in his very first shot of the night. He turned and stood, facing Lance.

"Regardless, Alex knew what she was getting into when she married me, I need to be in LA and she has to deal with that."

Lance shook his head, "You've got to be the dumbest motherfucker I know. You don't know what you have."

"I know exactly what the fuck I have, okay?"

Lance shook his head, "If you did you wouldn't take Alex for granted like you do, she puts up with more bullshit than she needs to from you. I don't know why the fuck she stays with you."

"Because she loves me that's why and you need to get over it."

Lance laughed, "Here we go again."

"Yeah, here we go… you still can't get over the fact that she picked me and not you."

"Alex and I have been friends since my freshman year in college, nothing more nothing less."

"But you wanted more until she met me, your older, the more dapper brother. It still eats you up that she chose me while you got thrown in the friend box."

"Yeah, okay bro… I think you need to focus on keeping Alex from leaving your ass then some ancient history bullshit."

"Yeah?"

"Hell yeah," Lance threw down his stick. "I'm done with this stupid ass conversation. I'm going back to the party. I suggest you go talk to Alex."

As Lance walked out of the man cave, Malcolm just laughed.

He laid the stick down on the table and walked back over to the bar to pour himself another drink. He stood there contemplating everything

Lance just told him and as much as he didn't want to accept it, the truth hurt, bad.

Malcolm downed yet another drink and needed to blow off some steam and he knew exactly how he was going to do it.

# TWENTY

"Can I come in?" Sylvia dipped her head into the theater room to see Alex laid out on one of the reclining plush theater chairs.

Alex turned her head, glancing Sylvia's way as she forced a smile across her disheartened face, "Sure, why not?"

"You know there's a party celebrating you out there right?" Sylvia said softly, closing the door behind her and walking toward her friend.

"Unfortunately. I am no longer in the partying mood."

Sylvia took a seat in the recliner next to Alex, "Well the good news is, Lacey is doing a great job at entertaining everyone while you and Malcolm take your, ah, break."

"Ha, is that what you wanna call it?" Alex shook her head.

"The bad news is, she is drunk off her ass."

"Jeez, how embarrassing."

Sylvia smiled as she reached out to grab her hand, "You wanna talk about it?"

Alex turned her head back straight; as she closed her eyes, a small tear fell out of her eye, "I don't know girl, it's just so hard ya know? I try to be that perfect wife and—" Alex wiped a tear away, shaking her head.

"Maybe that's the problem Alex, you try to be perfect and… no one is perfect, no one," Sylvia said, feeling a sense of self in that statement.

"Yeah, that's what I have to keep telling myself."

Alex's hand drops from Sylvia's hold as she sat up grabbing a tissue to wipe her face dry, before leaning back again in the chair. Silence fell between them.

"Alex?" Sylvia broke the silence.

Alex turned to face Sylvia, "Yeah?"

"Why do you stay?" Sylvia knew it was a bold question, but she had to know.

Alex looked away before turning her head back, shrugging her shoulders, "I love him and… I know he loves me."

Sylvia took a deep breath, shaking her head slowly, "Yeah, but love is relative in my book."

Alex smiled, "Love is also hard work and an investment of two people who want to make it work."

"So you think Malcolm really wants to make it work?" Sylvia asked, despite already knowing what Alex might say. She knew that her opinion was vastly different than the opinion she'd formed about him and their marriage.

"Deep down I do, I really do. I know he has a lot of issues and I understand at times where he is coming from."

Sylvia bit her lip. She knew Alex was a unique breed, and in a class of her own. She grimaced, closing her eyes and fought off the thoughts of what went down between her and Malcolm. She wanted so badly to tell her best friend but couldn't - at least not now, not while she was feeling so down and vulnerable. Sylvia asked herself, *when would be the right time?* She could only hope and pray when it was that her friend would forgive her and hope they could work it out, no matter how painful it was.

"What are you thinking?" Alex asked, pulling Sylvia out of her trance.

Sylvia smiled at Alex and reigned in her emotions, "That... that I love you."

Alex smiled, reached out to grab her hand, "I love you too." Alex sat up, "Why are you being so emotional lately? Talk to me, hon, what is really going on with you?"

Sylvia felt her emotions grabbing her like a human clamp and squeezing them tight as her body responded with a hard cry.

"Oh Sylvia," Alex stood, bending over Sylvia and hugging her, "Hey, what's going on girl? You're shaking!" Sylvia wept in Alex's arms. "Please tell me what's wrong?"

Sylvia pulled back, looked deep into Alex's eyes. *Oh god. I can't do it, I just can't.* She took a deep breath, then, "I'm pregnant and I don't know what to do."

"Oh my goodness, you are."

"I am."

Alex laughed, "Yes you are, girl."

This statement pulled a needed laugh out from Sylvia, "I knew you knew..."

Sylvia rubbed the tears from her face as Alex leaned over to her chair, opening a compartment on the side of it and pulling out more tissue, this time for Sylvia as she wiped away her tears.

"I don't know what to do..."

"Have you told Lance?"

"Oh God no, that would really have him running for the hills."

Alex sat down on the arm of her chair, crossed her right leg over her left, "Honey, like I said earlier, he just may surprise you."

Sylvia let out a small laugh, "I know you said that, but it's one thing to speculate and another to know the reality."

"Yeah, this is true, but we both know how sensitive he is, God knows I wish my husband would have gotten some of that DNA, but, well he didn't and I'm... slightly okay with that."

That statement pulled a well needed laugh out of both of them.

Alex looked up then back down shaking her head, "But Lance, Lance loves you, he truly does, and maybe this is what he needs to finally do the right thing, man up and stop it once and for all with his disappearing act."

Sylvia knew what Alex was inferring. She knew Lance better than anyone, even his own family, for the mere fact that she is not self-centered but very empathetic to others around her, especially ones that love her.

"I don't know, I'm just so confused. I do love him but he won't listen to me, ya know?"

"Well, maybe this will get him to listen, maybe this will get him to change."

"He claims he wants to make it work, but I just see us repeating the same old patterns, and we both know he needs professional help."

"Shit, don't we all?" Alex laughed at her own response, "Although this little gem may give Lance the push he needs to get that help."

"Yeah," Sylvia said agreeing but still skeptical.

"I think you need to tell him, tonight."

"Tonight? I can't."

"Why not?"

"I just... it just doesn't seem like the right time."

"It's never gonna be the right time, hon, ever."

Sylvia ran her fingers through her brown curls, "I'm not ready to be anyone's mom, Alex."

"Who is? But you will be a great one and guess what? I will be right there the whole way. Auntie Alex won't ever let you down."

Sylvia squeezed her eyes shut, nausea skipped back and forth in her tummy. She loved Alex like a sister but couldn't shake the guilt of what she had done, *fuck*. Sylvia couldn't hold on to this guilt any longer. "Alex?"

"Yeah, hon."

Sylvia stared deep in her eyes, "I um, I need to tell you something."

Sylvia turned to see Alex wearing a look of concern on her face. "What's going on?"

"You know I love you more than anyone on this earth."

Alex smiled, "Aww, I love you too."

"And I would never do anything knowingly to hurt you?"

"I would hope not, what's going on, you're scaring me a little."

A tear dropped from Sylvia's eye, *I am so sorry, I didn't mean to do what I did, intentionally, I know you may never forgive me but I have to tell you what I've done, how I've betrayed you with your husband, Malcolm.*

Sylvia played the scenario in her head. "Oh god, I um…" Sylvia took a deep breath, sat up and turned to Alex, "I um, I…" as she let out her breath laboriously between her lips, Sylvia swallowed, then, "I… I know your stance on abortion and I didn't want you to be mad at me if I decide to go that route," Sylvia said.

"Oh sweetie, come here," Alex opened her arms as Sylvia stood and they embraced, tightly. "Sylvia, you don't want that, I know you don't."

Alex rubbed her friend's back as she calmly spoke, "I know I've spoken my stance on abortion, yes, but at the end of the day, I still support free choice because we all have to live with that choice, it was given to us to use as we see fit in our own lives."

Sylvia hugged Alex a little tighter, not wanting to let her go, wishing she could turn back the hands of time. Wishing she would have never coveted another woman's husband, never foreseeing the future bond she would hold with his wife, her now best friend.

"Whatever you do, I will support you one hundred percent because no matter what, I love you unconditionally."

Alex's last words tore a hole in Sylvia's soul as the tears fell again from her eyes uncontrollably.

"My love for you can never be wavered by anything, you got that?" Alex said as she pulled back from Sylvia, looking her deep in her eyes.

Sylvia couldn't speak, the lump of guilt in her throat was suffocating her and anything she could ever say to her best friend. Sylvia knew in that moment that she would have to live with this guilt for the rest of her life.

# TWENTY-ONE

Malcolm, headed up the stairs turning the corner to see Nikki at the end of the hall. She turned, and they held a stare. Malcolm walked towards Nikki with purpose and in that moment couldn't control the anger, frustration and jealously that was brewing inside him. He looked around to make sure the coast was clear before opening the door of the hall closet, pulling Nikki inside with him and shutting the door behind them.

"What are you doing Malcolm? Let me out!" Darkness covered their bodies as Nikki fought to free herself from Malcolm's grip, but his strength overpowered her.

The smell of leather and suede tickled their senses. Malcolm didn't say a word, only pressed his body against hers as his hand slid between her legs. Nikki jerked, falling through the coats against the back wall of the semi-walk-in closet.

"Are you crazy, Malcolm? Your wife—"

"Like you give a fuck about my wife," Malcolm said. He dropped his voice down to a whisper, bending down to get closer to her ear. "I need to fuck you, now," Malcolm commanded as his hand continued up

Nikki's leg as it ventured towards her gateway; the smell of her pussy intoxicated him as he massaged her clit through her panties.

"Malcolm, stop… I have to get back to my date."

Malcolm didn't respond to Nikki's request, he was on a mission and he could give two shits about her date. "Tell me this shit doesn't excite you…" Malcolm whispered, his hand continuing to roam under her skirt. He could feel her wetness soaking through her panties as he slowly grabbed the silky fabric with his two fingers, sliding them down until Nikki relented, helping him wiggle them off.

She moaned and Malcolm smiled, licking his lips in anticipation for what was about to take place. He felt his manhood pulsating as his erection pushed against his zipper. He thought about Alex, what he was about to do. He knew he loved his wife more than life itself but as a man his natural instincts were to roam and conquer. Coupled with his frustrations of the night, this moment with Nikki in his closet was inevitable.

Malcolm turned Nikki around as he pushed his erection hard against her ass while sliding his hand around her waist and under her skirt, he circled her throbbing clit as he felt her wetness cover his fingers.

Nikki let out another moan as Malcolm kissed the back of her neck, biting her shoulder then quickly turned her around to face him. He took his fingers off her pussy and slid them in her mouth.

Her breath was heavy and moans were inviting as Nikki sucked her juices off his fingers. Malcolm dropped his hand back down and continued to massage her swollen lips with his thumb, sliding two fingers in and out of her. "You want me to stop now? Just say the word..."

Malcolm continued to massage her throbbing clit as he continued to slid his two then three fingers slowly in and out of her, Nikki's head fell back, "Oh my God."

Malcolm smiled, "Is that a yes, I didn't hear you…"

Nikki continued to release slow moans each time Malcolm slid his fingers inside of her then out and over her clit before repeating the motion over and over.

"Tell me how much you want me. Tell me you can't stop thinking about me. Tell me you want me right here right now. Tell me."

"Fuck you Malcolm," Nikki said. She reached down and unbuckled his jeans, Malcolm shifted to the right then left as they fell to the ground and rested around his ankles.

Nikki pulled up her skirt as she straddled her right leg around Malcolm's waist.

"Hold up," Malcolm reached down inside his pocket. He pulled out a condom, tearing it open with his teeth and sliding it down his erect penis. Malcolm then cupped his hands under her ass raising Nikki in the air as she wrapped her left leg around him as well. Their mouths connected with urgency as their tongues danced a familiar dance. Nikki moaned again, as Malcolm pulled her body into his with his left hand while guiding himself inside her with his right. Nikki let out another low whimper as Malcolm entered her.

"Oh, shit you feel sooo good," Malcolm murmured as he thrusted forward as they fell hard against the back wall of the closet.

Nikki's pussy welcomed Malcolm like it was born to be there. It swallowed his dick as Malcolm felt a rush of sensation shoot through his body like a bullet.

"Oh god, fuck me hard..." Nikki pleaded.

Malcolm pushed into Nikki as she pushed back, feeling all of her around him, feeling ecstasy racing through him. Malcolm moved his hips, slow, then fast, fast, then slow. Malcolm felt every muscle in his body flexing then releasing as he built up a satisfying rhythm. They continued to climb the ladder of pleasure only to stop when they heard voices passing by.

"Oh shit," Nikki let escape from her lips.

"Shhhhh. Don't say a word, don't move," Malcolm said in a low, almost undetectable tone in Nikki's ear.

They stood motionless as the voices got louder, closer, "Are you looking for the bathroom?" Alex said just beyond the door of the closet they were in.

"I am, is this it?" The male voice on the other side of the door questioned as he began to turn the knob of the closet door.

"Actually this is the closet. The bathroom is down the hall to the left," Alex continued directing her guest unintentionally away from the closet door where Malcolm and Nikki continued to stand motionless.

"Great, thanks," the male voice said before his footsteps faded away followed by Alex's.

Nikki let out a breath she had been holding in, "Holy crap."

Malcolm nervously laughed and he began his slow thrust once again, building to a faster pace. Their mouths devouring each other between each movement, between grunts, breathing in each other and out. Nikki squeezed her legs tighter around Malcolm's waist as he cupped her ass moving faster and faster. A slapping noise circulated around them, bouncing off the four tight walls.

"Oh baby," Nikki breathed into Malcolm's open mouth as their tongues continued to taste each other."

"You like that?"

"Yes, oh god, yes," Nikki answered between her clenched teeth. "Yes."

Sweat fell between them, quiet moans escaping from them. Malcolm went deeper, Nikki groaned louder, their mouths bound together as their tongues tasted each other, their moans becoming one.

Malcolm continued to push into Nikki, again and again, as her juices ran down his leg, he felt his climax coming fast, felt Nikki contracting around him, knew they needed to be quiet but it was so very hard.

"I'm coming baby," Nikki pushed out between soft panting breaths.

Malcolm felt his orgasm racing alongside of hers, the muscles in his back flexed, sweat dripped down the slope of his back and into his pumping buttock. Faster he thrusted, sweat mounting, heart beating faster and faster. One last push and, "Oooooh my god," they came together in unison and in ecstasy.

Both panting, and deeply satisfied, Malcolm's body felt weak as he dropped Nikki's legs down to her side, his body leaning against her, their chest expanding and contracting together, the heat from their bodies rising around them.

"Damn," Malcolm said as he slowly pulled up his jeans, wiping the sweat from his face, "You good?"

"I'm great," Nikki said as she planted a small kiss on Malcolm's lips. "Hey baby?"

"Yeah?"

"I love you."

Silence filled the closet.

"Malcolm, did you hear me?"

Malcolm heard Nikki loud and clear, a little too clear for his liking, this was so typical Nikki to throw around the L-word right after a damn good orgasm, fucking up his high.

"Come on, we better get back before they notice we are gone."

"Hey, Malcolm, have you seen Nikki?" Malcolm turned to see Davis walking up behind him as he adjusted his pants.

Malcolm slowly shook his head as he casually scanned the living room, "Can't say that I have, maybe she bounced on you."

"Nah, she wouldn't do that, not to me at least."

*Yeah, don't be so sure,* Malcolm thought as he looked away then back at Davis. "Right, of course, I see you got it like that."

"Well ya know, a brother's got it going on," Davis said as he smiled, tapping Malcolm playfully on his shoulder with his fist.

Malcolm shook his head, "Maybe check the backyard area?"

"Cool," Davis said as he turned then quickly swung back around, "Oh, before I forget, I um, I didn't mean to overhear your conversation with Alex about the distribution deal." Malcolm gave Davis a displeased look. Davis threw up his hands, "You know I wasn't *trying* to hear your conversation, but you two weren't exactly keeping it on the low, low."

"Right, what's up?"

"I actually may have a hook up for you in the distribution department."

Malcolm felt himself calming down, and raised an eyebrow, "Really?"

"Yeah, some cats I know from Ohio have a distribution company that apparently has a connection with AMC."

Now Malcolm's interest was really piqued. "Word?"

"No doubt, I mentioned you to them a while back while we were shooting and they were very interested in what you were doing."

"Okay," Malcolm continued to listen as his eyes glanced behind Davis to see Nikki, then quickly shifted his attention back to Davis.

"Listen, if you like, I can set up a meeting and have you guys meet."

"You'd do that for me?"

"Anything for the great Malcolm Monroe. It's nothing, really. I mean come on, we gotta look out for each other, right?"

Malcolm smiled, "Exactly man." Malcolm's eyes diverted over to where Nikki was now standing. "Ah, I think I see who you are looking for."

Davis turned to see Nikki then back at Malcolm, "There's my fine ass date," Davis said before offering up his hand to give Malcolm a pound.

"So I will hit you up about the meeting."

"Cool man, thanks a lot," Malcolm said as he watched Davis make his way over to Nikki. He wrapped his arms around her waist as Nikki glanced back over towards Malcolm as he gave her a quick wink.

# TWENTY-TWO

"There you are. Where were you? I've been looking for you for over twenty minutes now."

Malcolm looked up to see Alex walking his way. "I was in the game room."

"Really? I looked in there…"

Malcolm looked around, making sure Nikki was nowhere in sight. Instead of answering Alex's question, he changed the subject. "I see the party is somewhat over." Malcolm continued to scan the room before making direct eye contact with Alex.

"Yeah, I mean, we didn't exactly make it comfortable for our guests to stick around, now did we?"

Malcolm shrugged his shoulders, "Yeah, I guess," he said reaching for a bottle of water. He opened it and drank half of the pint-size plastic bottle.

Alex took a seat on the stool in front of their center island, "I think we need to talk about what happened."

Although Malcolm felt a lot calmer now, he wasn't trying to revisit their previous conversation. "What's there to talk about?"

"There's a lot to talk about, Malcolm, do you even wanna hear my side?"

"Not really because I'm not moving, Alex," Malcolm said, finishing off the bottle of water and tossing it in the trash across the room.

Alex took a moment, looked down, then back up. She hated what was about to come out of her mouth, but knew that sometimes you had to pick your battles. "I don't want to fight."

"Well maybe you should have thought of that before you sprung this news on me."

"I won't take that job in the Bay."

"Wow. So you were actually considering it?" Malcolm said, his eyebrow arched and lip turned up.

Alex sat back and folded her arms, "I was."

"I don't know why you would be thinking that. We agreed that LA would be our home base," Malcolm said. His eyes passed Alex to see Nikki walking out into the living room, taking a seat on the couch. She smiled and winked towards Malcolm. Malcolm looked away from her and back at Alex.

"Like I said, Malcolm, it's no longer an option."

"Great, then we can move on with our regularly scheduled program." Malcolm turned and as he started walking out of the kitchen when he heard,

"We also agreed to have children," Alex said realizing *this* was the battle worth picking.

This stopped Malcolm in his tracks and he felt an annoyed twitch shoot through his body, "Excuse me?"

"On our wedding night, we sat across from each other and carved out a plan of action for our lives. One of those things was for us to have two children. Don't you remember that?"

Malcolm swallowed, not wanting to dig up the past, especially that past. Frustration and exhaustion escaped between his lips, "Yeah, I um, I remember it, but that was a long time ago, Alex. Things change… people change."

"That's true, but a promise is a promise and you made that promise to me."

Hearing this, Malcolm was almost tempted to tell Alex to take that job in the Bay if that meant he could get out of having a baby.

"Having a child is a big adjustment and I am not prepared for that. That's the honest truth, Alex."

"I know it's a big change, but in life change is inevitable," Alex jumped off the stool and walked towards Malcolm. She took one last step in closer to him, held his face in her hands, "Baby, we talked about a family together, a future, and what I want more in life is to have children. Jobs will come and go, a family is forever, our family. It's time."

Malcolm felt the tightness return to his chest. He knew how persistent Alex could be, and knew she would continue to broach the issue until she got her way. Malcolm touched Alex's hands that lay on his face and gently pulled them away.

"I know what we talked about but I think we should wait... just a little bit longer," Malcolm said, trying to keep his cool.

Alex's shoulders dropped along with her facial expression, but she wasn't about to give up. "Baby, I'm forty years old and I don't want to wait any longer to have a child. It has to be now." Her voice was much firmer this time.

Malcolm took a few steps to the side, closed his eyes, then opened them as he stared Alex's way, "Well you're just going to have to wait," Malcolm continued out the kitchen. Alex followed close behind him, she wasn't done.

"Why are you doing this? Why can't you for once just agree with what I want? Why is it always a battle with you? Huh? We agreed to have children, so why are you doing this to me?" Alex's built up frustration thickly coated every word that flew out of her mouth.

Malcolm stopped, "I know what I said, but things... things are different now," Malcolm threw back.

"How? How are things so different now than when we first got married?"

Malcolm walked a few steps forward before turning back toward Alex. "I don't know, Alex. All I know is that I can't exert any more energy for a child, I just can't. My career—"

Alex threw her arms up in an "I give up" gesture, "Of course, your career. It's like you love your career more than me."

"That's not true, but you know how much my career means to me and what it means to me to get back on top."

"Geez-us Christ, don't I know, the whole freakin' world knows, and guess what? You will. What I'm trying to make you see is that we can have both. People do it all the time. They have a family and a career. It's not impossible."

Malcolm took a few steps away from Alex and felt frustration fighting to take over, "Alex just stop okay? Stop trying to convince me it could work, because it can't."

"It can."

"It can't"

"Why not?" Alex threw back.

"Because I never wanted any children in the first place."

Malcolm's body jerked as those last words fell from his lips, he didn't mean to say that out loud, his anger and frustration got the best of him, all of him. "Shit."

Alex felt the words hit her like an internal blow to the pit of her stomach. It took her breath away, all of it. She cupped her mouth to muffle the cries from seeping out, but that didn't stop the tears from running down her face.

"Why would you say that?" Alex said, breaking eye contact with Malcolm, on the brink of a bigger breakdown. She pulled her hand away from her mouth as her words fell from her quivering lips.

Malcolm took a step towards Alex, "Alex I didn't mean that, I just --"

Alex put her hand up, as she took a step back, "Stop, just stop. Do you even want to be in this marriage, Malcolm? Do you even love me?"

"Alex don't start talking crazy. Of course I do…" Malcolm reached out to touch Alex, but she pulled away.

"I'm not trying to hurt you," Malcolm said trying his best to explain, "I just… I just envisioned my life so much differently than what it has become. I know it's partially my fault. Ever since my father died, I've just been trying to put together the pieces that led me to where I am today and it's not fucking adding up."

Alex shook her head, felt her hands starting to tremble, turned around then back towards Malcolm, "Nothing in life adds up to what we ever want, but that doesn't have to keep us from trying. You cannot put your life on hold until what you think should happen happens, it just doesn't work that way. I am here now, but you can't even open your eyes to see the beauty right in front of you."

Alex wiped the tears from her face as she stood a little taller, "I'm willing to fight this fight with you, you just have to be willing to meet me half way, and stop putting your present life on hold for what you think should be your future."

Malcolm stood still, very still. He opened his mouth but nothing came out. He looked away, then back at Alex. "I just... I..." Malcolm folded his arms then unfolded them, and looked away.

"This is just great." Alex turned and walked out the kitchen, disappearing from Malcolm's sight.

"Shit." Malcolm took small deep breaths as he looked up to see Nikki staring his way.

# TWENTY-THREE

"Some party, huh?"

Lance opened his eyes to see Sylvia standing over him as he sat on the couch with his head laid back and his feet up. "Definitely one for the record books."

"Yep."

An awkward silence fell between them. Lance sat up, dropped his legs to the ground and scooted over a few inches making room for Sylvia. Sylvia saw the inviting gesture and took a seat next to him.

"I think we got off on the wrong foot tonight and I wanted to be the first to apologize."

Lance looked over at Sylvia, a nonchalant expression covering his face. "Okay. Apology accepted."

Sylvia raised her eyebrow and let out a chuckle, "That's all you have to say?"

Lance shrugged his shoulders, "What else is there??"

"I don't know, maybe you could try and muster up an apology of your own."

Lance looked around as if trying to recall a reason to give one, "For what? All I did was show up with a friend and you did your best to make sure she didn't stay past cocktail hour."

"I didn't tell her to leave," Sylvia shot back, defensive.

"You didn't invite her to stay," Lance replied, his mouth curled up on the side.

"Are we gonna do this again?" Sylvia returned her own stern look.

Lance put his hand up in defense. "Fine."

"Good." Sylvia looked away, looked at the few remaining guests mingling amongst themselves at the party. Sylvia looked back over at Lance who was now looking straight ahead.

"It was a nice party while it lasted, huh?" Sylvia's attempt at small talk.

Lance surveyed the room, "If you ask me, it never started."

Sylvia rubbed her stomach, thought about what Alex said, thought this could be the perfect opportunity to say what she needed to say.

"Lance, listen I need to talk to you about something—"

Lance turned to her, "Yeah, about what?"

Sylvia shifted where she sat just inches from Lance, looked down in her lap, felt a nervousness swirling in her building momentum as the thought of telling Lance she was pregnant with his child started to become a reality. She cleared her throat, then as she opened her mouth she heard a loud crash with a high-pitched voice coming from inside the house… she looked at Lance who sprung to his feet upon hearing the noise.

Before Sylvia had a chance to follow suit, she saw Vivian charging through the French doors headed straight for her intended target... Lance, she hoped.

"Oh shit," Sylvia gasped. She didn't know who looked crazier. Vivian who was raging, or Lance's expression as he watched Vivian quickly make her way towards him.

"You bastard!" Vivian spewed Lance's way as he took a steps back to accommodate her unexpected, yet, deranged arrival.

"Vivian, what the hell are you doing? Calm down."

"No, you calm the fuck down!" Vivian yelled, her face beginning to turn a crimson red, starting on her cheeks but quickly spreading over her entire face.

Sylvia took a few steps away, *this couldn't be residual anger from the whole wife soon-to-be-ex revelation*, she thought.

"Why are you tripping?" Lance threw back at her.

"Maybe these will give you an indication," Vivian said throwing a pair of pink satin panties Lance's way. Sylvia watched as they hit Lance's chest and fell softly down to his feet, covering the tip of his right shoe.

*Nope, this was definitely something new,* Sylvia continued in her head as she took a few more steps away from Lance just in case Vivian started throwing out assumptions that they were hers, which in her experience would be followed by swinging arms.

There was no mistaking the fact that Vivian was pissed beyond consolation and Sylvia was not about to be a casualty to her rage.

"I found them in your car, Lance," Vivian added, the hostility thick in her voice.

Lance looked down at the pink silk panties laying on his shoe then back up at her. The few guests who were still in the party, including Malcolm and Alex had now migrated outside and in earshot of the verbal outburst.

"I don't know what you're talking about. I don't know how those got in my car." Lance said, kicking the panties to the side with one swift movement of his leg.

Vivian laughed shaking her head, "Well I have a big fucking clue, Lance. Would you like to hear it?" Vivian asked with both hands on her slim narrow hips.

Lance looked to the right then to the left, he wasn't sure how to answer that question and it was scribbled all over his face. Then a random guest in the background yelled out, "I do."

Vivian's stare was locked on Lance, "How about someone you're fucking." She boldly threw out the accusation, "And I have an inkling as to who it may be," glancing over at Sylvia and back at him.

"Okay, time out." Sylvia made a T with her hands. "I don't do cars darlin', so don't even look this way."

"Funny how quick you were to let me know you were his wife," Vivian said.

"Soon to be EX," Sylvia quickly threw back.

Vivian didn't acknowledge Sylvia's statement, instead turned and locking in on Lance, glaring at him as she examined every inch of him, monitoring his body language hoping to catch him in a lie, "Who is it Lance? Who are you fucking? Because those panties are not mine."

Lance shifted, twisted his mouth, as his eyes narrowed then glanced Malcolm's way. Malcolm held his stare firm, unaffected, uncaring. In that moment Lance knew, without doubt, he knew what was now going on.

Lance slowly shifted his attention to Alex then back again at Malcolm who held his ground before he licked his lips, taking one step towards Vivian, "I have no idea how those panties got into my car," Lance said in a very calm methodical voice. He gave Malcolm one last look. One last chance to do what he should but wouldn't.

Vivian slowly shook her head from left then right, "After five months of dating, that's all you can say?"

*Five months*, Sylvia scoffed to herself. She knew Lance was lying about his relationship with Vivian.

Lance paused, contemplated his next words, weighed his options in his head, he could end this now once and for all, but he knew Malcolm had a lot more to lose, much more. Lance shrugged his shoulders. "Yeah, I guess so."

"You are such an asshole, you know that? A fucking asshole," Vivian said as her eyes filled with tears. "Matter of fact, it's over, don't call me, don't text me, and unfriend my ass on Facebook Lance. Fucking-over-you."

Lance looked back over at Malcolm who now wore a smug smile on his face as he shrugged his shoulders and shook his head, then back at Vivian who was already headed for the front door.

"Vivian, wait! Can we just talk about this, in private?" Lance said catching up with her.

"What's there to talk about Lance, you were unfaithful *and* you lied about it to my face. Where do we go from here?"

Vivian turned again and headed out the door. Lance thought for a minute, then followed after her.

"Vivian hold up." Lance headed through the double white French doors, past a few lingering guests, Malcolm and Alex as he approached the foyer. He caught up with Vivian about to walk out the front door.

"Come on Vivian, seriously."

Nothing could stop her now, she was gone. Lance tried one last time as he yelled her name through the door, "Vivian."

"Yo, let her go man."

Lance turned around to see Malcolm standing behind him in the foyer with his hands tucked in his pockets.

"What?"

Malcolm waved his hand towards the door, "Just let her go. You gonna go running after a jump off? Not like you're serious with that."

Lance felt his anger hit a breaking point and his emotions got the best of him, all of him. "Man fuck you. It didn't matter what I was gonna do, I lied to her for yo ass," Lance said with a raised tone.

Malcolm laughed out loud, "Well look at it as a feather in your cap of good deeds."

Lance slammed the front door, "Fuck a good deed man and fuck you, I am so tired of always covering for you."

"Is that right?"

"Hell yeah." Lance felt the vein in his neck pulsating.

Malcolm stepped closer to Lance, and grabbed his arm tight, "Do you really think I give a shit? She was a jump off, I did *you* a favor." Malcolm glared into Lance's eyes.

They were almost nose to nose, "And don't forget, you owe me motherfucker," Malcolm continued.

Lance's heart started to beat fast, too fast. He jerked away from Malcolm, "After tonight I think my debt is paid off. In full."

Malcolm grabbed Lance again, "It ain't paid off until I said it's paid off."

Lance jerked away from Malcolm again, hard, "I'm outta here. If you think I'm gonna sit here and act like nothing happened when you know good and goddamn well, it was *you* fucking some chick in my car and not me and you were the sloppy one for leaving those panties behind."

A loud gasp bounced between the four egg shell covered walls in the small foyer before falling on Malcolm and Lance's ears alerting them to turn around where Alex stood, *mortified.*

"Oh shit," Lance blurted out.

Alex turned and ran out of the foyer, up the stairs, down the hall and into her bedroom, slamming the door behind her. The sound ricocheting back down to them.

Malcolm turned to Lance, with an enormous amount of hate in his eyes, a long intense stare off began, neither one saying anything but much tension building.

"You fucking bastard," Malcolm lunged for Lance as their bodies slammed together before they both hit the ground, vibrating the floor, knocking over a vase on the near shelf nearby sending it crashing to the marble floor. They began to wrestle with each other, struggling back and forth, neither one gaining much of an advantage.

Everyone moved to try and pull Malcolm off Lance, and while Lance was a lot stronger he still managed to hold his brother off.

Lance stood, "What the hell is wrong with you?" Lance shouted.

"What the hell is wrong with me? What have you done?" Malcolm said in between vigorous breaths while two people held him back. "I cannot believe you just did that yo."

"I'm sorry bro, if I had known she was there I would have never said anything. I wasn't thinking," Lance threw back.

Malcolm stood, pushing the two people holding him off and began pacing. He tried to get his thoughts together, wondering exactly what the fuck he was going to do now. He turned to look at Lance, "I'm gonna lose her this time... because of your ass."

Lance shook his head, tucked back in his shirt that was pulled out during the tussle, still trying to catch his breath, "Yo, this has nothing to do with me, I was just a small vessel caught in your storm of vast destruction."

"Seriously spare me the mellow fucking dramatics, because of yo ass I need to figure out what to do," Malcolm said as he paced back and forth, rubbing the back of his neck.

"Let me talk to her."

"And say what?" Malcolm looked up at Lance, a heavy sigh escaping through his lips, "I think you've done enough."

"Hey I'm just trying to help," Lance threw back.

"Helping would have been keeping your damn mouth shut."

"Just be honest with her,"

Malcolm looked up, holding a stare with Lance, "Really, is that really your solution here?" Malcolm shook his head laughing out loud as his mind were drifting back to a memory, a memory triggered by this moment.

*Malcolm and Lacey entered into the familiar front door and stood in the foyer when they heard, "Get out, you bastard!" The rage of their mother's voice rang through the second floor of the house before traveling downstairs where they stood frozen.*

*A five-year-old Lacey clung to a nine-year-old Malcolm, who tried to act as if he was not affected but, he was. Another crash sent a jolt through his body as Lacey clung tighter to his waist.*

*"It's okay, Lace, they are just talking."*

*"No they're not. They're fighting. They're always fighting," Lacey said, looking up at Malcolm. Malcolm knew his little sister was getting older and wiser to her surroundings and she was correct. They were always fighting.*

*Another crash, and this time it was something that shattered. A few seconds later, Langston Monroe appeared at the top of the stair case, dressed in a pair of black slacks and crisp white shirt. "Just calm the hell down, Eleanore, you gonna hurt someone."*

*Eleanore appeared behind him, disheveled and hurt, tears streaming down her face and her hair a complete mess. Wearing a silk robe and only one house slipper still remaining on her foot, she stood at the top of the stairs screaming at her husband.*

*"If you don't leave this house, God help me!"*

*Langston Monroe shook his head and casually approached Malcolm and Lacey looking down at them as if everything were normal.*

*"Are you leaving Daddy?" Lacey asked, her voice shaking.*

*"Yes, baby girl, but I won't be gone for long. Just enough time to let your mama cool off a bit."*

*"Why don't you just tell her the truth?"*

*Langston looked over at Malcolm, took a few steps towards him, "Because women don't want to hear the truth."*

*Malcolm looked away, as what his father said resonated within him before looking back up at his father.*

*Langston put his hand on Malcolm's shoulder, "You be the man of the house while I'm gone, you hear?"*

*"Yes sir," Malcolm slowly nodded his head with uncertainty in his eyes.*

*"I mean it, I'll be back in a few days, so you need to step up."*

*"Yes sir."*

*Langston took a deep breath, looked back up to where his wife stood who was still fuming in anger. Shaking his head, he moved out the door, closing it behind him.*

*Malcolm peered out the side glass door to watch his father walk down the stairs and get into the black town car. As the town car pulled off, he felt a sense of relief. But it quickly turned to sorrow as he looked to see Lacey in tears. His mother walked back into her bedroom and slammed the door.*

"Malcolm?" Lance yanked him out of his trance.

"What?"

"It's not too late to come clean, I know she loves you yo."

Malcolm folded his arms, "There's nothing to tell." A smile crept across his face, "nothing happened."

Lance shook his head. "That's how you're gonna play it, huh?"

"That's how it is," Malcolm said with great confidence.

"I love you, bro, but you got a lot to learn. You can't keep running, it will catch up to you eventually."

Malcolm chuckled to himself, "Not if I run fast enough it won't."

Lance swallowed hard, "I'm done." He turned and walked away.

Malcolm stood alone in the foyer, looked at the broken glass that laid on the floor beneath him. Yeah, he knew Alex was mad, but also knew that if he gave her enough time to cool off, everything would be back to normal soon enough.

# TWENTY-FOUR

Lacey needed to get some air and since the party was pretty much over, she decided to head out to the front and take a few minutes for herself. The thought of a cigarette floated in her mind as she had to remind herself the reason she gave it up, her voice was more important than her nicotine addiction.

Instead, Lacey reached for a pack of eclipse gum and popped the tiny square into her mouth shaking it out from its blue packaging. The taste of fresh peppermint washed over her tongue and taste buds as she focused on the white Lexus pulling up in front of Alex and Malcolm's house.

She watched as a woman stepped out the car, closed the door, set the alarm then walked towards what appeared to be the house. Lacey stared at the woman walking her way, the familiarity of her face, her walk, that attitude.

The moment Lacey realized who this woman was, she almost choked on her gum.

"Jana?"

"Well hello Lacey." Jana's greeting was accompanied with a pleasant smile.

Lacey shifted as she sat on the top step of Malcolm and Alex's porch. *What the hell was Jana doing coming to Alex and Malcolm's home?*

"Are you at the right place?" Lacey asked with a rising attitude.

"The home of Malcolm and Alex is it?" Jana semi inquired.

"Yes it is. So once again, are you at the right place?"

Jana laughed as she looked down then back up, "I see we are not quite there yet."

"There?"

"Friends."

"No." Lacey threw out, "Why would we *ever* be friends…. at all?"

Jana's smile faded as she took a few steps closer, stopping just a few inches from Lacey, "Well I guess that's your call."

"It should be."

"Great, well um I am here to pick up a friend, so excuse me," Jana said as she stepped past Lacey sitting on the top step.

Lacey tilted her head. A friend? *And who would that friend be?*

"Hey you made it," Lacey heard Reagan's voice behind her as she stepped out the front door. "I just got your text that you were a few minutes away. Let me get my coat, and say goodbye to my cousin, Alex."

Jana looked down at Lacey then up at Reagan, "Cool, I'll wait here."

"Beautiful, I will be back in a sec."

Reagan winked at Jana as she stepped back into the house. Lacey stood avoiding any more eye contact with Jana as she headed into the house behind Reagan, leaving Jana on the porch, alone.

Lacey followed Reagan to the back of the house and into the guest bedroom. She noticed Reagan diligently searching for her belongings amongst the few remaining coats spread across the dark brown duvet on the bed. Lacey pushed the door ajar, standing in the doorway.

"What is it now, Lacey?" Reagan said without looking her way.

"You're leaving?" Lacey said with folded arms as she leaned against the frame of the doorway.

"Looks that way."

Lacey carefully pushed herself up as she took her strides into the room closing the door slightly behind her, "Listen, I came in here to apologize."

Reagan looked up, "Apologize for what?" She looked back to continue the search for her jacket.

"I don't want us to fight, I really would like us to at least be friends," Lacey said, hoping her jealously of seeing Jana wouldn't rear its ugly head.

Reagan found her jacket, slid it on and turned to face Reagan, "That will be very hard for me, Lace."

"Well for me too, but clearly we want different things in life. Why can't we just agree to disagree?"

Reagan's head lurched back then forward upon hearing Lacey's last statement, "Agree to disagree? Here's a tip, that only works if the parties stay true to their feelings."

Lacey knew exactly what Reagan meant, but chose to ignore it. "I am... true to my feelings."

Reagan took a deep breath as both eyebrows shot up then down, "Fine, you wanna be friends, let's be friends. I gotta get going," Reagan buttoned the top two buttons of her jacket taking a few steps past Lacey.

"I actually know that woman out there, you know," Lacey said, her way of stalling Reagan for her selfish need.

Reagan stopped turned back to Lacey, "Okay," Reagan said, shrugging her shoulders, "and?"

"And I just thought you should know is all," Lacey said, trying to stay neutral, but it was a struggle.

"Great, thanks," Reagan shot back.

"So are you guys like, a couple?" Lacey felt herself blurt out before she had a chance to catch herself. She hated when she got this way and it only happened with Reagan.

Reagan looked up, sucked her teeth, tilted her head slightly to the left, "She's a friend, okay?"

"Just… a friend?" Lacey continued her subtle interrogation.

"I don't feel comfortable talking about this with you," Reagan said as she reached for the door knob.

"Why? We're friends... right?" Lacey continued, not backing down.

Reagan chuckled, "Sure Lace, friends." Reagan opened the door slightly.

"Did you also know Jana is my road manager?" Lacey said, her one last attempt to keep Reagan from walking out that door.

"Yeah, she told me that too."

"Cool," Lacey said with a smile on her face. "Although I'm sure she didn't tell you that she hit on me after our meeting today?"

Silence fell between them, with a long uncomfortable beat.

Reagan rolled her eyes, "Okay, this isn't going to work."

"Why because you are dating my road manager who is trying to fuck me?"

"Jesus Christ Lacey, seriously, everyone doesn't want you, okay?"

Lacey shrugged her shoulders, "Not according to Jana."

"Whatever Lacey, if that gets you through the night, roll with it okay?" Reagan tried to leave once again, Lacey took a few steps towards her, softly grabbing her arm, "Okay, I'm sorry, I'm sorry. I didn't mean that. Please, don't go." Reagan stopped, looked down. "I just didn't think this would be so hard," Lacey said.

"What's so hard?"

"This, us, seeing you," Lacey swallowed hard, finally succumbing to her feelings, "I fucking miss you and —" Lacey ran her fingers through her hair. "And I'm so confused right now."

Reagan still yet to make eye contact with Lacey as she looked away, trying to find her thoughts, her feelings, trying to stay calm. "I know Lace, it's not easy, but you have to want to make it work."

"I don't know how to do that."

Reagan finally looked up, "Well that's one thing I can't do for you," Reagan pulled her hand away.

But Lacey wasn't done, not yet. She took two more steps towards Reagan, grabbing both hands with hers, "I'm so confused because…

because I feel so safe when I'm with you, but in my world that shouldn't be right."

Silence fell between them. Reagan couldn't let go of her hands and felt her stomach balling up. Lacey moved in closer to her as Reagan met her half way.

"I just can't stop thinking about you…" Lacey said softly, kissing Reagan on her cheek, then neck.

Reagan breathed out a deep sigh, "Me either."

Lacey continued to kiss Reagan's neck before venturing to her lips. Reagan slowly pulled back before surrendering to her sexual urges and her strong love for this woman as she slid her arms down Lacey's side and around her back, pulling her closer to her. Body to body, they began to kiss slowly, building to an uncontrolled passion.

Reagan pulled away, "Lacey, we can make this work, I promise. Just say the word and I am all yours."

Lacey let out a small moan as she continued to kiss Reagan.

"Tell me you want to be with me," Reagan pled between breaths.

"I do…" Lacey took a deep breath, "I do..."

They continued to kiss when Lacey pulled away, "but… I can't just cancel my wedding now. The invitations have already been printed."

Reagan jerked back. "Oh my God, what the hell was I thinking? What am I doing?"

"That we can still be together?" Lacey proclaimed.

"No we can't."

"Why not?"

"Because I'm nobody's side piece, that's why." Reagan dropped her hands from around Lacey's waist.

"I don't see it that way."

"You wouldn't," Reagan stepped away from Lacey. "You're not doing this to me again, I am finally moving forward and I'm not going to let you knock me back again. Nope, not gonna happen." Annoyed, Reagan turned and began to head out the room.

"Reagan, wait."

"What now?" Reagan barked at Lacey.

"I love you."

Reagan stopped, as an exasperated chuckle slipped from her lips. She turned towards Lacey as they locked eyes,

"No Lacey, you only love yourself."

Reagan swung back around and headed out the room leaving Lacey at a loss for words.

Reagan took a few steps before she bumped into Nikki who was about to enter the room. "Sorry." But Reagan kept going. A devious smile spread across Nikki's face as she watched an annoyed Reagan head down the hallway and out of sight.

Nikki had been turning the corner when she heard two female voices. She was just about to enter the bedroom to grab her belongings and head home when she saw Reagan and Lacey in a serious lip lock. Nikki wasn't too surprised after watching the two of them interact all night. They were like two scorned lovers trying to avoid each other's breathing space.

So when Reagan came bustling out of the room practically knocking Nikki to the floor, Nikki knew this was something she needed to keep under her hat. Or should she?

Nikki made sure the coast was clear before heading back into the bedroom to find her purse and coat where she saw Lacey adjusting her top. Lacey looked up as Nikki threw on a pleasant, *I saw nothing*, smile.

"You're Lacey Monroe," Nikki ventured to say.

"I am," Lacey said in a dry tone. Clearly her mood was still affected by her run in with Reagan.

Nikki extended her hand. "I didn't get a chance to introduce myself with all the drama tonight."

Lacey nodded her head, "Yeah, my brother def knows how to bring the drama." Lacey said as she shook Nikki's hand.

"I recognized you from your videos on YouTube. I'm a big fan by the way."

"Thanks. How do you know Alex?"

"Oh, I just met her tonight, I came with Davis."

Lacey gave Nikki a confused look.

"He was in Malcolm's last film, the tall boyish looking guy with the short curly hair."

"Ah, Right. Cool."

Randolph walked in. "There you are, we should get going."

"Of course." Lacey looked over at Nikki, "Nikki is it?"

"Yes."

"This is my fiancé, Randolph."

Nikki smiled to herself. "Hello."

"Well it was nice to meet you, Nikki."

"Yes, it was great to meet you as well. Hey if you ever, you know, perform anywhere local, let me know, I would love to hear you in person."

"I'm actually going on tour soon. I can let Malcolm know my dates here. I'll comp a few tickets for you."

"That would be awesome." Nikki smiled.

Lacey threw a goodbye smile Nikki's way before she exited the bedroom with Randolph.

"Wow," Nikki said to herself out loud as she leaned against the wall, a wicked smile stretched across her face.

# TWENTY-FIVE

"So what were you and Reagan talking about?"

Lacey felt a chill zigzag through her body as Randolph's question hit her like an unexpected left jab.

"What?" Lacey decided to act vague, almost dismissive, hoping not to give off what she was feeling in this moment.

Randolph slid on his suit jacket without taking his eyes off her. "I saw you two talking before you walked to the back of the house."

Lacey felt her face grow flushed and felt the knot return to her stomach. She swallowed hard then, "Oh right, we must have just decided to leave at the same time, so we headed back to get our coats together."

"Oh, okay, well it seemed as if you two were discussing a delicate matter."

"Just small talk. Her friend is actually my road manager. Small world, right?"

Randolph gave Lacey an easy smile, "Right." He buttoned up his jacket, smoothing out each sleeve separately.

Lacey looked his way, as Randolph focused his attention on himself, she took an internal sigh of relief, until...

"How well do you know this... Reagan?" Randolph looked back her way.

Another awkward question that had Lacey feeling uneasy and unsettled. Did Randolph see something between the two of them? Was he throwing out feelers? Or was her conscious just getting the best of her? Either way, Lacey didn't like the direction of this conversation.

"I met her a few times through Alex. She's Alex's little cousin you know."

"Yeah, that's what you said when you introduced her."

"Right," Lacey said but not recalling saying that.

"So you two are just acquaintances, then?"

"Yes, honey, where are you going with this?" Lacey said, she had enough of the passive aggressive interrogation already.

"Nowhere," Randolph gave another easy smile, "You ready to go?"

"Sure, let me just go say my goodbyes, if I can find Alex and Malcolm."

"Great. I'll wait for you in the car."

"Perfect," Lacey threw back as she gave Randolph a faint smile.

As Lacey watched Randolph walk out the front door, she took a deep breath, and felt anxiety filling up inside. She walked to the kitchen, saw an open bottle of white wine, grabbed a glass out of the upper cabinet and poured herself a full glass. She took a few quick sips before dumping the rest down her throat.

Placing the long stemmed glass on the island, she scanned the living room and dining room for Alex and Malcolm, but they were nowhere to be found. She thought about heading upstairs but decided to send a text.

After tonight's events, it was better that way. She was sure to catch up with them tomorrow.

Lacey pulled the front door shut when she spotted Reagan and Jana standing by the street talking in front of Jana's Lexus. Their body language screamed more-than-friends and they were not trying to hide how they felt for each other. Lacey felt a jealous gnawing in the pit of her stomach as she rolled her eyes and headed to where Randolph was waiting for her in their truck.

She opened the passenger door and slid into her seat, adjusting herself as she pulled her seat belt across her chest clicking it in place. A faint jazzy melody floated out of the speakers as Randolph sat in silence staring out the front window at Jana and Reagan.

His head slowly moved from side to side partnered with a deep loathing sigh, "Gay people disgust me. When will they learn that they are living in sin?"

The mere mention of the word *sin* made Lacey's throat dry up, made her wonder what he would think if he knew what she had done, who she had done it with. Her intimate, yet sexual, on-again-off-again relationship with a woman rushed to the forefront of her thoughts. Lacey pushed her guilt and conflicted morals to the side and did her best to rationalize her sexual behaviors before speaking her next words.

"No more than anyone else in this world," she managed to push out.

Randolph stopped and looked at her, his stare serious, his intent strong. "Lacey, the bible undeniably states in Leviticus (18:22): *You shall not lie with a male as with a woman; it is an abomination.* Period." He turned his head back towards Lacey and Jana as he spoke his last words, "Unrepentant homosexuals have no place on this earth."

Lacey swallowed, realizing she was walking on thin ice, realizing, unbeknownst to him, he was referring to her and her relationship with a woman, Reagan to be exact.

Lacey smoothed out the bottom half of her dress with her hands, felt the sweat in her palms sink into the blended cotton, "Then wouldn't it be fair to say that he hates unrepentant murderers and embezzlers as well?"

Randolph's head snapped back Lacey's way, "No, it's not the same!" Randolph threw out her way, his stance accompanied with flared nostrils and a growl. Lacey couldn't believe what was coming out of his mouth with such venom. *Was he serious right now?*

Lacey sat in silence as she contemplated her next thoughts, choosing what to say carefully. She turned to Randolph and put her hand on his arm just as he was about to shift the gear to drive.

"If you really think about it, we are all living in sin in one way or another, right?"

Randolph's eyebrows pushed together as a concerned looks flooded his face. Lacey pressed on, trying to make her point, "I mean, why is a homosexual act frowned upon ten times more than one who murders, steals or covets one's spouse?"

Randolph took his hand off the gear, "I don't think I like where you are going with this, Lacey. What *they* are doing is wrong." He points in the direction to Lacey and Jana, to bring home his point.

"Yeah, I got that." Lacey swallowed, looked away, then back at him with careful intent. "I'm just saying why should we care what they do behind closed doors? It's really none of our business."

"It's God's business and that is who counts. Should I remind you in Leviticus (20:13): *If a man lies with a male as with a woman, both have committed an abomination; they shall be put to death; their blood is upon them.*"

"Okay, enough with the bible quotes, I get it." Lacey felt herself getting way too emotional, she took a deep breath. Randolph raised an eyebrow as Lacey pulled back a bit. "I just think people have the right to do whatever they want with their own lives as long as it doesn't affect anyone else," Lacey continued.

"Not as long as the bible states what is morally right and what is morally wrong."

Lacey paused, not wanting to continue the conversation. She knew it would be a never ending battle and she knew Randolph would not let up until she was on his side.

"Okay, um, do we really have to talk about this now? I'm tired and I really want to go home and go to bed. I have a long day tomorrow."

Randolph looked out the window towards Reagan and Jana, then back to her, "I need to know if you are for homosexuality and that lifestyle or against it? If you are, we sincerely need to have a bigger talk about *us* as couple."

Lacey stared out the window, caught a glimpse of Reagan and Jana playfully talking, touching, flirting. They looked happy, content. Lacey felt the gnawing knot of jealously growing bigger with each minute that passed as she watched their flirtatious interaction. They finally jumped into the car and drove away as Lacey thought back to when she had that feeling of butterflies in her stomach whenever Reagan would come into the room, or simply look at her a certain way, even touch her with a tender touch.

She recalled moments of their lovemaking, sensual, passionate, and at times animalistic, feeling herself getting wet at the thought of it. She squeezed her eyes tight trying to push the images away, far away. She tried to substitute them with her here and now, and her new life as Mrs. Randolph Sanders. She thought about her obligation to her family, her fans, and society to do what they all thought was supposedly the right thing - settle down, have children, do what her mother always told her to do...

So why couldn't she stop thinking about Reagan? Why couldn't she stop thinking what she was doing was a mistake?

"Lacey? Lacey?"

"Yes," Lacey turned back slowly towards Randolph as she was pulled out of her trance.

"You didn't answer my question. Where do you stand when it comes to homosexuality?"

Lacey turned and looked out the window once again to where her past once stood then back at her fiancé where her future now sits, "My stand?" Lacey put on a soft smile, "Homosexuality, it's wrong, very wrong."

# TWENTY-SIX

"Alex, come on babe, open the door, we can talk about this."

Malcolm leaned against the door as he lightly knocked with two knuckles, wasn't sure what to expect when she finally let him in but he had to try. "This is all just a ridiculous misunderstanding. Alex, Alex." Malcolm dropped his forehead against the door rocking it from side to side, as he cursed Lance's name in his head. His brother could never keep his trap shut. It was his fault that he was in this mess.

Malcolm knocked once again, "Please baby. Just hear me out." Malcolm tried the chrome polished door knob only to confirm that it was indeed locked. Malcolm's hand dropped down to his side before up to his head where he raked his fingers through his hair, then down the back of his neck.

Malcolm pushed himself up from the door, turned taking a few steps away only to swing back around when the bedroom door suddenly swung open. His relief mixed with excitement dissipated quickly as soon as he noticed Sylvia walking out of the bedroom.

"What were you doing in there?"

Sylvia closed the door softly behind her, "Talking to my best friend."

Malcolm's face scrunched up as if he had just bitten into a ripe lemon, "Please… I think you'll want to look up the definition of what a *best friend* is before you start throwing around that title so freely - especially when it comes to Alex."

Sylvia ignored Malcolm's comment and moved to walk past him. Malcolm sidestepped to the left and blocked her way. "Where do you think you're going?"

"I'm going home, Malcolm. It's been a long, event-filled night and I'm exhausted."

"It sure has Sylvia, but I'm not letting you leave until you tell me what you two *best friends* were talking about in there." Malcolm held a hard stare with her.

Sylvia's eyes narrowed, "That's none of your business," Sylvia tried to walk past Malcolm once again, only to see him take another sidestep to block her way for the second time.

"I'm not playing this game with you," Sylvia said, her tone harsh. She didn't know how else to make it clear that she was fed up with his games.

"Did you finally find a way to turn my wife against me once and for all, huh?"

Sylvia laughed, shaking her head in disgust, "Astonishing idea, but you've pretty much done that on your own."

"What? She's gonna leave me now over some stupid bullshit? Is that what she told you?"

"I would. Matter of fact I would have left your ass a long time ago."

"Well we both know Alex is an intelligent woman, she knows where she needs to be and that is with me."

Sylvia took a step back as she folded her arms in front of her chest, eyes narrow to slits, "It's sad how this sense of entitlement you wear like a badge will finally do you in, you mark my words."

Malcolm's smile spread across his face like a blossoming flower, "Well, you just keep in mind that if I go down, we all go down." Malcolm demonstrated with his hand a plane crashing accompanied with the explosive sound effects.

Sylva cleared her throat, gave Malcolm a half grin, "You don't get it do you? *This*, is not about me. *This*, happened way before us. *This*, is something you brought into your relationship from your own fucked up life. That woman in there loves you and you're just too damn self-absorbed to see it."

Sylvia stepped closer to Malcolm and dropped her voice down to a whisper, "Yes, it's unfortunate what happened between us and if I had known then what I know now it would have never have gone there, ever. We all make mistakes, but mistakes are always forgivable if one has the courage to admit them." Sylvia stepped back, "Now move the fuck out of my way."

Malcolm grinned and took another step to the side, this time in the opposite direction as to allow Sylvia to move past him.

Sylvia headed downstairs as Malcolm watched her leave thinking about what she just said. A deluge of painful memories from the past shot through his mind, flashing before his eyes, stinging his soul. He shook his head, trying to ignore the memories she'd forced back in his life.

He stood firm and yelled down the hallway to a long gone Sylvia, "Fuck you Sylvia!" Watching her go, he lowered his voice, commenting to himself, "Damn shame she is such a bitch, with a fat ass like that. What a waste."

Malcolm quickly directed his attention back to the bedroom door and took a deep breath. Throwing on his most sympathetic look, he moved into the room seeing Alex sitting on the bed. She'd changed from her party clothes into Juicy Couture aqua blue sweat pants and a white v-neck fitted tee pulled tight against her chest. Her bloodshot eyes glanced up at him then back down as she remained quiet and still.

"Hey you," Malcolm threw out softly as he closed the door behind him, he walked closer to the bed as he sat down on the edge of it, carefully keeping his eyes pinned on his intended target.

"Crazy night, huh?"

Alex kept her gaze pinned to the covers that lay beneath her.

"Come on, Alex, you can't stay mad forever, right?" Malcolm reached out to touch Alex's bare foot, but she quickly drew her legs in tighter to her chest.

Malcolm pulled his arm back as he placed his hand on his leg as he rubbed up and down his slacks, took a deep breath, "Do you need more time? I can come back..."

Malcolm dropped his head trying to find some kind of eye contact with Alex, searching for a glimmer of forgiveness, "Alex?"

Alex stayed silent, Malcolm slowly nodded his head before standing, "Fine I will come back when you are ready to talk."

Malcolm turned to leave the next words that fell from Alex's mouth paralyzed him.

"I met someone."

Malcolm stopped dead in his tracks; he felt a wave of nausea consume him as his whole body felt instantly weak. Unsure that he'd heard correctly, he slowly turned back towards Alex who was now staring at him with unapologetic rage in her eyes.

"What did you say?"

"I met someone," Alex said, with a hint of venom.

Malcolm swallowed hard as he felt beads of sweat instantly multiply on his forehead and nose like rabbits. His mouth opened to speak but nothing came out. For the first time in his life, he was speechless. The sheer impact of the single statement from her was ricocheting through his entire body.

Malcolm managed to stay still, watching Alex's pupils turn a dark black, as they stared intensely into him.

"I was hurt and I had no one to turn to. I wanted to feel loved and you made me feel like I was undesirable. You made me feel like nothing."

Malcolm finally exhaled as he started to breathe deeply. The pulsating muscles in his neck felt like a valve waiting to explode. *What the fuck is Alex saying to me? What the fuck is happening right now*? His mind began to race as he began to feel dizzy. He began to hyperventilate.

Alex dropped her feet to the floor and slowly stood, her voice shook as tears ran down her stone cold face. "You hurt me sooo deeply, that you will never know and I wanted to make you feel the pain that I felt, and understand the hurt I experienced."

Malcolm grabbed his side, the pain he felt in this moment made him stammer, made his words jam between his thoughts and the need to express what he was feeling, made him want to wreck something, anything.

"Did you hear me Malcolm? I met someone."

Malcolm shook his head, felt dizzy and confused, he put his hand up, pointed to Alex, "Who the fuck is it?"

"You don't know him."

Malcolm slid his sweaty palm down his thigh, balling it into a fist, then looked up at Alex, "Really? Try me, Alex. Do you work with him? Did you meet him on your commute home? Is he a mutual friend? Who the fuck is it?" Malcolm's voice rose with each question.

Alex didn't move from the spot where she stood, "Like I said, you don't know him," Alex said, her voice completely calm, even though her eyes were filled with tears.

"Stop fucking lying to me."

Alex let out a cry-filled laugh, "Really Malcolm, are you serious right now?" Alex took a few more steps towards Malcolm. "I have no need to lie to you. Unlike you who have been lying to me all these years."

Alex wiped her tear-drenched face, "I was the fool that was faithful to your ass Malcolm, as faithful as they come, but I've come to learn that

that shit gets old, very old, especially when my very own husband looked me in my eyes and swore to me that he would never *ever* lay hands on another woman again, but you did." Alex's sorrow quickly turned to anger, "So like I said... I met someone."

Malcolm felt his body giving out, the jealously he felt, the images that he began to summon of his wife with another man took everything out of him. He fell down onto the bed, his mouth felt dry but the rage continued to build with every word that hit him from Alex's mouth.

"Did you... did you fuck him?"

Alex paused, folded her arms, looked away, and back at Malcolm, "No, I haven't."

Malcolm felt his anger subside somewhat, not much but enough to ask the next question, a question that would surely send him into a rage, "Do you want to?"

Alex held a stare with Malcolm, then, "Yes," she said simply.

"***Aaaahhhhhh***!" Malcolm let out a loud frustrated scream, as he leaned over tossing over the night stand near the bed sending the lamp, books and everything on it crashing to the floor.

"You thought I was just gonna sit around while you had affair, after affair, after affair? No, those days are over."

"Shut up," Malcolm yelled out as he dropped to his knees from the bed trying to keep the tears and the rage from overpowering him, but it was too much to handle, too much to consume at once. The memories of the sorrow and pain he felt from what his dad did to his mom raced to the forefront of his mind, something he swore he would never do, is doing, has done. He looked up at Alex, and felt a sense of guilt mixed with rage and topped off with agony.

"I don't want to be like this, like him. I am so sorry." Malcolm slowly stood, "What have I done to you, to us? What have I done? I don't want to lose you."

Alex was now in tears.

"Tell me what to do to make it right, to make this better, us better." Malcolm said as he put his hand on his head, as the pain of his childhood peppered this moment.

"Tell me, please Alex."

Alex took a few steps towards Malcolm and stopped when she was mere inches from his face. "I don't know what to say anymore." Alex walked past Malcolm and he watched her move into the bathroom and shut the door behind her.

Malcolm stood in silence, not knowing what to do or what to make out of Alex's statement. He spun down in a circle, like a dog chasing his tail, like a man chasing a life he let slip right through his fingers.

Alex shut the door behind her as she slid down to the floor muffling her cries with both hands. She felt an agony like no other, hurt and despair. Why did she tell Malcolm about meeting another man? Was Sylvia right? Would that make him change his cheating ways? Would that make him become the man he was supposed to be?

Alex dropped her head into her hands, replaying in her mind her conversation with Sylvia that lead to this moment…

*"I don't know what do to Sylvia, but I'm sure I can't do this anymore." Alex looked over at Sylvia from across the bedroom. Alex stood by her closet as she unzipped her dress, letting it fall to the floor. She then disappeared into her closet only to reappear slipping on her aqua blue sweat pants.*

*"I know, sweetie, and you shouldn't have to," Sylvia said as she sat on the edge of the bed.*

*Alex grabbed her white form fitted T-shirt from her top drawer of her eight drawer dresser and pulled it over her head. She then walked over to the bed and sat down inches from Sylvia, "I mean, come on, two affairs, how many more? Am I going to find out about another one next month?" Alex shook her head, attempting to hold back her tears.*

*"He sat there and told me to my face that the first woman was nothing and it would never happen again." Alex couldn't hold back any longer and began to cry, "And he did."*

*Sylvia moved in closer pulling Alex into a warm embrace. "I'm so sorry sweetie."*

*"What am I going to do?" Alex said as she sat back, wiping her tears. "I am like out of options here."*

*Sylvia took a deep breath, "Do you want to stay in this marriage?"*

*Alex looked away, felt a push pull with her soul, the love she felt for Malcolm still remained in her heart even though the pain was never ending. She was so confused, but in that confusion she knew the love for him was still there.*

*"Yes, I do."*

*"Then tell him you met someone."*

*"What?"*

*"The one thing I've learned in my years of dealing with men, especially the monogamous cheaters like Malcolm, is you need to do a little shock value. Give them some of their own medicine."*

*Alex let out a nervous laugh, "What are you saying?" She thought about Xavier, thought about what could be if she wanted it, but did she want that?*

*"You want Malcolm to straighten up, let him know there's some competition, let him know you're no longer gonna just wait around for him to come home to you after he's done fucking some women. Tell him you met someone."*

*"So let him know I am having an affair?" Alex threw out, wondering if Sylvia knew about her two-month fling with Xavier, something that she would never divulge to anyone.*

*"No, no, not in the midst of an affair, that's stooping to his level, just that you met someone and there is the possibility of you leaving him for that person."*

*"You think that would really work?" Alex questioned Sylvia's motives.*

*"Honey, men are competitive by nature, that's what drives them, that's why they watch sports like it's the last thing on earth. Let him know there is a chance he will lose you forever, and let him know it will be to another man."*

*Alex stared at Sylvia, not sure of how to take the information she was giving, but knew, at this point she was out of options. Alex wiped the last tear from her face, this was a lot to handle but even more to digest.*

*"So you really think this will work?"*

*Sylvia leaned back, crossing her arms, "Yes."*

**A**lex leaned her head back against the bathroom door, going quiet as she tried to listen for Malcolm on the other side. She began to wonder if what she did had worked. Would he fight for her? Most of all, would he stop his cheating ways?

Alex took a deep breath, stood up as she looked at her reflection in the mirror, her bloodshot eyes and tear-streaked face stared back at her. She dropped her head, listened for movement on the other side of the door, nothing. Alex turned on the faucet, splashed a few handfuls of water on her face, grabbed a towel and buried her face in it.

She dropped the towel down on the counter beside her, turned, took ahold of the doorknob and slowly turned it. Her heart sank down to her knees as she wasn't sure what the future held, not sure how this would all end, her marriage, her life, but it was time to find out.

# TWENTY-SEVEN

Sylvia stepped off the last two stairs onto the main floor when she spotted Lance coming her way, but she wasn't in the mood to talk. In fact she was pretty well all talked out.

"Hey," Lance said as he met her at the bottom of the staircase.

Sylvia stopped, smiled, "Hey, what's up?"

Lance's eyes divert up the stairway to where she just came then back down to her, "You um, you were up there talking to Alex."

She took a breath, attempting to keep her poker face, "Yeah, I was."

"Cool. How is she?"

Sylvia bobbed her head as she ran her fingers through her hair, "She's gonna be fine," she said giving as little information as possible to him. Lance had already proven what a big mouth he had and she was not looking to let her scheme with Alex backfire so soon.

A surprised look flashed across Lance's face, "Really? All right..." That surprised look quickly morphed into a look of despair, "Not sure if I can say the same about my brother."

Sylvia knew she could write a novel just from that comment alone, but she decided to keep it short, "Well we both know what a piece of work he is."

"Yeah, that's for damn sure." Lance stared at Sylvia. She wasn't sure where he was going with this semi-awkward conversation, but she was ready to get the hell out of this house.

"So, you leaving?" Lance finally spit out.

"I am, you need a ride?" *Dammit*, that was the last thing she meant to say but her pregnant fatigued mind was getting the best of her.

Lance gave Sylvia a sly smile, "Yeah, I'm not falling for that, but that's not why I asked."

*Thank gawd.* "Oh, okay." Sylvia said as she shrugged her shoulders. She grabbed her coat off the back of the chair, slid it on. She was on a mission to get home before the Tonight Show.

"You in a rush?" Lance said this as if he were trying stall her. It almost sounded to Sylvia that he wanted to talk about something.

"Kinda, I'm a little tired."

"Long week?"

"Very," Sylvia threw back, hoping Lance would get the hint and happy he didn't take her up on her offer to drive him home.

"Oh okay," Lance said sounding a bit more nervous this time as he swayed from left to right before reaching into his inside sports jacket and pulling out a white envelope, "Here." Lance handed Sylvia a small envelope.

Sylvia adjusted her purse on her shoulder before looking at the envelope then taking it slowly from him, "What is this?"

"The divorce papers you have been hounding me for, they are all there, all signed. I even dotted all the I's and crossed the T's."

Sylvia's mouth fell agape as a strong sense of repentance and relief smashed together like a campfire s'more flooded her thoughts. She smiled, cleared her throat then opened the envelope, "O-kay, although, you don't have a single I or T in your name."

Lance smiled at Sylvia's humor at this delicate moment, "Yeah, I know, glad you got the joke."

Although the last type of emotion Sylvia was trying to display was joy, she was able to throw back her half smile, "Well glad to see you still have a sense of humor in all of this," Sylvia said. She unfolded the papers and just stared at them, the nausea she thought had checked out for the night, quickly checked back in as the familiar saying popped in her head, *Be careful what you wish for,* before she glanced up at Lance with warm eyes, "Are you sure you want to do this?"

Lance arched an eyebrow, as his body lunged back, "Why would you ask me that? You have been bugging me for weeks to sign them."

Sylvia waved her hand in the air as she was swatting away a fly, "Right, of course, I just—" *wanted to see if you had a change of heart if you knew I was pregnant with your child,* Sylvia rehearsed to herself, trying to muster up the nerve to actually say it out loud.

"But you are right," Lance said.

"About what?"

"I have no business in a relationship. I gotta get my shit together, really together. Maybe then you will help me get out of this mess I'm in."

Sylvia hated when her advice came back around like a fucking boomerang when she wanted it to keep on flying north. "Well, I didn't really think—"

"I mean, I can't even keep a jump-off around, right?" Lance said, cutting off Sylvia's last sentence.

Sylvia dropped the papers to her side, "Lance that wasn't your fault."

"Yeah, I know."

"So why did you cover for him?"

Lance threw his arms up, "Shit, I don't know, he is still my brother and let's face it, he has a hell of a lot more to lose than me right now."

Sylvia looked away, then back at Lance, wondered how this conversation would be going if that crazy bitch hadn't come storming back into Alex's party waving week-old panties in the air like they were bounty sheets, who does that?

"I guess so," Sylvia said realizing she had missed her window of opportunity, window of what could have been. She folded the papers, sliding them back into the envelope. "I'll um, I will get these to you by end of the week." The last words that fell from her mouth hurt as she swallowed hard to contain her emotions.

"Cool," Lance said.

Sylvia stepped past Lance, hoping he didn't see any emotions from her, this unborn baby was turning her into an emotional mess, "Well I guess I will see you around then."

"Sure."

Sylvia was almost home free when she heard…

"Hey wait."

Sylvia turned back around, "What's up?"

"Right before the big Vivian blowup, you were about to tell me something?"

Sylvia felt her heart drop down to her stomach and bounce back up again. Was this the sign she was waiting for, was this her opportunity to finally tell Lance what she had been hiding for the last two months, "Yeah, I was just gonna say…" Sylvia let out a warm smile, "right after—"

The sound of a ringing cell phone halted the conversation, Lance quickly realizing it was his.

"Dammit sorry, hold on, sorry," Lance said, retrieving his phone from his pocket then glancing at the display. "Oh shit, it's Vivian." Lance's eyes grew big as saucers, "You think I should get it?" Lance directed the question Sylvia's way.

"I um, I don't know," Sylvia said, not sure why Vivian would be calling now but even more unsure as to why Lance would ask *her* advice on how to handle it.

His phone kept ringing, "Shit, okay, I should take it, right?" Sylvia shrugged her shoulders.

"Okay, I'm gonna take it," Lance swiped the bar across the phone, "Hey Vivian?"

Sylvia looked up then back down. This had to be the most uncomfortable moment of her life. *Yep it was definitely time to go*. Sylvia raised the divorce papers as he mouthed to Lance stuttering on the phone to Vivian, "I'll be in touch."

"Yeah," Lance threw back over his shoulder, before walking out of her earshot.

Sylvia walked out the main door of Alex and Malcolm's home, closing it behind her, breathing in the night air as she headed to her car.

She carefully slid into the driver's seat of her car, managing to keep her nausea from getting worse. Sylvia closed the door behind her as she leaned her head back onto the headrest and began to give serious thought to what had been in the back of her mind since she realized she was actually pregnant. With her busy schedule and crazy sleep patterns, Sylvia thought she was just under the weather, but when her sudden sickness lasted 3 weeks, she knew she needed to pay a visit to her doctor.

Sylvia reached into her purse and pulled out her cell phone and hit a number on her speed dial. After a few rings and a long outgoing message, Sylvia pulled the phone away from her face before pressing it back to her ear. *Was she really contemplating this? An abortion?* Before she had a chance to answer herself, a beep prompted her to leave a message.

"Hi, um, this is Sylvia Batista, leaving a message for Dr. Anderson." Sylvia paused, letting out a soft burp, swallowing the bit of liquid that came up with it, "Could you please give me a call back at your earliest convenience. Actually, it's very important that I hear back from you. Thank you."

Sylvia hit end, threw her cell phone down on the passenger seat, slide her hand across her belly, laid her head back on the head rest and exhaled the night away.

# TWENTY-EIGHT

Malcolm sat alone in his empty kitchen trying to process what just happened and who this dude Alex *claimed* she met was. He shook his head as he sipped from a half empty beer bottle trying to calm himself, trying to figure out what the hell to do.

Malcolm squeezed his eyes shut, and hated knowing how closely he'd begun to resemble his father. He hated how his life had evolved over the years and wished most of all that he hadn't ruined his marriage once and for all, resulting in Alex leaving him.

Malcolm didn't know if he could function without her around, leaving him to always wonder who she was with and who she was fucking.

His phone rang, shattering the silence. He reached in his pocket to retrieve it as he glanced at the display that flashed, NIK. Malcolm's initial instinct was to answer it, but no, not now, the last person he needed to be on the phone with was Nikki, not after what went down. Malcolm hit ignore and with the jerk of his wrist, dropped his phone onto the center island with a quick toss.

Malcolm turned his focus back onto Alex, worked to push the images of a man, any man with her out of his mind as he slowly lowered his head down onto the cold granite when he heard.

"Hey?"

He pulled his head up to see Alex standing just a few feet from him. He wasn't ready to talk, and definitely wasn't ready to hear any more of the nonsense she was spewing before. Malcolm looked away, and instead concentrated on the beer bottle in front of him. Anger had his words in serious lock down. He swallowed, took another swig of his beer, but still found that he had nothing to say.

Alex slowly walked to the opposite side of the island and just stood there, staring at him with her bloodshot eyes, with an expression before she said, "You have no reason to be mad."

Malcolm shifted in his stool, felt his anger surge from that comment, finally looked up at her, "Really, well, thank you for speaking for me, but I am fucking furious right now Alex."

Alex leaned over onto the island, propped her chin up with her hands, slowly shaking her head, "Welcome to my world."

Malcolm looked away, shook his head, hated being in this position, hated feeling the way he was feeling, knew he could change it with a single word and a hand full of action or could he? He wasn't sure what Alex's stance was, where she was coming from, what she was contemplating doing. He had never seen this side of her before and wasn't sure what the next move may be.

Malcolm took another swig of his beer, placed it back down on the counter, looked around the kitchen then back at Alex, "So you're still not gonna tell me who this guy is?"

Alex slowly shook her head from left, to right, "No."

Malcolm threw his arms up, leaned back in his chair, "Then why are you here? Why did you even come down here? To rub my face in it? To watch me throw another goddamn fit? What Alex? Please tell me because I am dying of anticipation here."

Alex leaned in a bit more, "I want you to appreciate what you have."

"I do appreciate you."

"Not if you keep cheating on me, no you don't."

"Tell me, is this your way of teaching me a lesson, huh? Is this your way of getting me back?"

Malcolm grabbed the beer by the neck, wishing it was that dude Alex had betrayed him with and not a frosted bottle. His anger was rapidly peaking to a level that he couldn't control, "Matter of fact, why are you even still here? Shouldn't you be on your way to see your new friend?"

"Is that what you want Malcolm, for me to be with someone else?"

Just hearing those last words made Malcolm's insides churn, made him want to hit something again. Something. Anything. Punch a fucking hole through it. His anger finally got the best of him as he sprung to his feet as his words exploded from his mouth, "What do you want from me Alex? What?"

Alex pulled up, matching Malcolm's intensity, bearing down for a verbal battle, "I want you to fight for me, I want you to stop me from walking out that front door into the arms of another man. I want *you* to once and for all to stop fucking around and be faithful to me, your wife. I want you to fight for me."

Malcolm looked away, felt his heart about to explode but also felt a sense of relief, a new beginning in a way.

Alex slowly walked around the island towards Malcolm as she continued to speak, "I know people make mistakes. I know we're not all perfect, but I am willing to forgive you again for the sake of us, our marriage." Alex stopped right in front of Malcolm, they were now inches from each other. They continued to stare into each other's eyes. Tears fell like raindrops down Alex's cheek as she reached out and gently rubbed Malcolm's face before running her finger over his lips, "All I want is for you to fight for me, for us."

A tear dropped down from Malcolm's left eye, as his lips began to quiver, "I will fight for you and I will love you."

"You promise?"

"I promise," Malcolm declared with all his heart.

Alex smiled as she dropped her body against Malcolm, "I love you so much."

"I love you too." Malcolm reached his arms around Alex's body as they embraced tightly. Malcolm squeezed his eyes shut and made a promise to himself this would never happen again, he was going to be the man he should have been years ago.

**A**lex jerked awake, her eyes struggled to focus in the dark that laid around her as she looked over at the clock that read 3:45. She slowly turned her head the opposite way to see Malcolm fast asleep while her mind replayed the events of the night less than twelve hours ago. A smile accompanied with a soft sigh spread across Alex's face. She could hardly believe Sylvia's plan *actually* worked.

Alex pulled herself up against their beige headboard before slowly pulling the covers back and dropping her bare feet down to the cold hardwood floor beneath her. The amount of wine she'd consumed at her party had triggered a thirst for water as she stood and quietly headed for the kitchen.

A motion light clicked on as Alex entered her state-of-the-art kitchen, she smiled as she tied her belt from her robe across her waist. This was one upgrade she knew she had to have and she wasn't willing to compromise to get it.

Alex headed around the center island to grab a small square glass from her upper cabinet before lifting a bottled water from the fridge. Alex broke the seal of the bottle and as she poured the water into her glass she heard three beeps coming from behind her. She stopped, turned and scanned the kitchen, but nothing, she then turned back around to pick up her glass only to hear the three beeps again.

Alex picked up her glass, took a long refreshing drink from the glass as her eyes spotted what was making the beeping sound.... it was Malcolm's phone. Alex slowly removed the glass from her lips, placing it back onto the counter as she stared at Malcolm's phone sitting on the center island. In that moment all the happiness she had accumulated from their mutual resolution started to slowly dissipate.

Alex swallowed and thought, *Should she look, one last time?* The silence around her engulfed her as the internal ticking in her mind only intensified her yearning to see who was on Malcolm's phone. Who was texting him at 3:45am? Alex leaned back against the counter, as she grabbed her water and took a huge gulp before placing it back down beside her. She wiped her lips, folded her arms, and just stared at the white iPhone begging her to pick it up.

*Don't do it Alex. This is a new start, a new beginning.* Her rational mind tried to weigh in on her internal conversation. *But what if? What if after all that had happened, Malcolm was still not going to change his ways.*

Alex shifted, breathed frustration through her lips, *Maybe I need to just give him time to break off all communication, he will, he promised.*

Alex's mind continued to battle. She ran her fingers through her short hair, squeezed her eyes shut only to have them pop back open from the sound of the beeps, "Shit," *Could it be the woman from the car, the woman with the misplaced panties, who is she? Do I know her? If I do, will that change everything?"*

Alex pushed herself up from the counter and took two small steps in the direction where the cell phone lay. She reached out to grab it but stopped just short as her hand hovered over the top before pulling it back, sliding it into the pocket of her robe. Alex turned, scooped up her glass and drank the rest of the water down before placing the empty glass in the sink. She glanced at the phone one last time, turned and began her exit out of the kitchen.

One step, two steps, and then three. She stopped, turned, then, "Fuck it."

She headed back into the kitchen and grabbed Malcolm's phone, swiping the bar to reveal three unread text messages from the same number, from a number that showed a name of NIK.

Alex swallowed, smiled, tried to keep herself calm but felt her hand begin to shake, her insides begin to melt as she tapped on the first message which read, "*Call me asap.*"

Alex closed that message as she taped on message two that read, "*I need to talk to you.*" Alex looked up, scanned the room, wondered who NIK could be, wondered if this was even a woman. She closed that second text message only to go to the third message, tapping on it to open it to read, "Fine if you can't call me back, I think you need to know something…" Alex felt a gulf of heat as her eyes read the last few lines of that third text… "I'm pregnant and you are the father."

Alex's hand went numb as the phone slipped through her fingers and down to the floor bouncing twice before landing next to her foot. She stared up the stairs where Malcolm laid, at least she now knew who the diamond earrings were for.

**THE END**
**To be Continued….**

**PRETTY LIVES UGLY TRUTHS**

(BOOK 2)

*Malcolm and Alex*

*(Coming Summer 2014)*

***PRETTY LIVES UGLY TRUTHS***

*(BOOK 3)*

*Lance and Sylvia*

*(Coming Fall 2014)*

***PRETTY LIVES UGLY TRUTHS***

*(BOOK 4)*

*Lacey and Randolph*

*(Coming Spring 2015)*

***WWW.KELLECOLLIER.COM***

**Author BIO**

**K. Elle Collier** is the writer of Amazon's best selling trilogy *My Man's Best Friend, Kai's Aftermath* and *Alana Bites Back.*

Released in 2011, *My Man's Best Friend* rocked the literary world with a hot new story and a strange new twist. Offering a stylish, unique contemporary voice, K. Elle's work marks a fresh new approach to the ordinary relationship story. With an honest ear for dialogue, and a knack for truthful, uncompromising storytelling, K. Elle pushes the envelope to discover intimacy and love in the most unconventional situations.

K.Elle Started her writing career off by participating in various esteemed writing programs such as: The Bill Cosby Writing Workshop, The ABC Writing Fellowship as well as Warner Bros. Comedy Writing Program, this in turn lead to a staff writing position on the CW sitcom Girlfriends. K. Elle later branched off to other avenues of writing such as screenplays and stage plays, where she adapted the best-selling novel 'Friends and Lovers' by Eric Jerome Dickey for the stage.

Her love for writing flowed over to novels in which she currently has 3 best selling books My Man's Best Friend (Book1) Kai's Aftermath (Book 2) and Alana Bites Back (Book 3).

K. Elle is currently working on a new book series "Pretty Lives Ugly Truths" along with other small projects to debut in 2014. Follow her on twitter @K_ElleCollier and like her on Facebook: Author K. Elle Collier

Made in the USA
Lexington, KY
16 August 2019